THE ORPHAN'S HOPE IN MANCHESTER

CATHARINE DOBBS
DOTTIE SINCLAIR

Copyright © 2025 by Catharine Dobbs & Dottie Sinclair

All rights reserved.

No part of this book may be reproduced in any form or by any electronic or mechanical means, including information storage and retrieval systems, without written permission from the author, except for the use of brief quotations in a book review.

PROLOGUE

1 *877*

Mother coughed again, and Florrie looked up at the sudden noise.

"Are you all right, Mother?" she asked.

"I'm fine, darling." Mother gave her a reassuring smile that seemed to waver. "You don't need to worry about me."

"Are you feeling sick again?"

Florrie hoped that wasn't the case. She had seen her mother like this ever since she could remember. Joanna Walsh had been one of those people who had a weak constitution. It wasn't her fault, but every time there was something wrong with the community and someone passed by with a cold, she would be unwell not long after. Neither Florrie nor her brother was like that. They were healthy, much like their father had been.

When he had been alive.

He had been dead for the past eighteen months, although it wasn't sickness that had taken him. A knife in a backstreet over unpaid gambling debts was the cause of his death. Florrie wasn't meant to know about that, but Preston had overheard some gossip with a few other children at the school. They seemed to have families moving in the same circles, and the older boys wouldn't stop talking about anything except the murder for the best part of a week.

It was as if they were taunting Preston and Florrie for their father being careless. Florrie knew it wasn't their fault, but it didn't help that people were talking about it behind their backs. She hated, even now, knowing that others were looking at her and her family and wondering if they were as bad as Father.

She hated gambling. Couldn't see the point in it all. And she wished everyone would just leave them alone.

They had enough problems, as it was, without having to deal with people looking down on them.

"Why don't you finish your homework, Florrie?" Mother suggested, her soft voice somehow echoing around the empty schoolroom. "The sooner I look it over, the sooner we can go home."

"But can't we go home now?" Preston asked. He sat beside Florrie, scowling as he twiddled his pen in his fingers. His skin was stained with ink. "This is boring. You can do the marking another time."

Mother sighed and shook her head.

"Much as I would want to, I would have to do this marking tomorrow morning before school, and you don't want to get up any earlier than you already do, right?"

Preston was silent with that.

"I thought not. It won't be long now, Preston. Just finish your homework, and then there's less to do at home."

"But..."

"And stop twirling your pen like that. You're staining everything around you."

Sure enough, when Florrie looked at her dress, she saw the sleeve and a bit of her skirt were splotched with ink. She shoved Preston sharply.

"Stop it!" she hissed. "You're ruining my clothes!"

Preston rolled his eyes, but he didn't argue back. Sulking, he dipped his pen in the ink and pretended to flick it at her before he started writing. His paper was splotchy as well, but at least it was readable. Florrie sighed and continued with her writing. Preston had been like this for a while now. He got easily bored and found himself more agitated with things that wouldn't normally bother him. He was a bright child but getting him to concentrate was another matter.

Maybe that was due to him getting older. He was ten now and growing up fast. Already, he was the same height as Florrie. He was going to be tall like his father, a man he'd adored.

Florrie felt awful for him. When someone you loved disappeared suddenly and it was discovered they weren't actually a truly good person, that could change someone's perspective on things. She had been horrified hearing all that and had put it down to gossip.

If it wasn't for the infrequent visits from a particular woman who made her feel cold every time she was in the room, she might've gone down that path. But the proof given to Mother, that Florrie had read over her shoulder, said otherwise. Her father had gambled so much that it would've taken him decades to pay it off with his salary.

And now it was hanging over their heads.

No wonder Mother was ill more often than usual. She was burning herself into the ground trying to keep up with it all. Florrie knew she was sick more than she cared to admit, and when she taught the children at the school it was almost a game with the other pupils to see when she would keel over first. But Mother kept going. She was trying so hard.

Florrie wished she could help.

"Right," Mother said, putting the last of her marking to one side in a neat pile. "That's done. Are you two finished?"

"I am," Florrie answered, and Preston sat up, nodding profusely. Glancing over at his work, Florrie was surprised to see that her brother had finished as well. He was very bright and could apply himself when he wanted to.

Mother had the patience of a saint to deal with him all the time. Florrie found it exhausting.

"Perfect." Mother beamed, now looking better than she had been earlier in the day. She stood up. "Let's go home. Fancy stopping off at the grocer's and getting some pork? He said he was getting some in, and he'd put some aside for us."

"You mean your new gentleman friend?" Florrie teased as they joined her at the door.

"No!" Mother blushed. "Nothing of that kind, Florrie, so don't be silly. He's just been helping us out with a few things that all."

"You have a gentleman friend?" Preston stared at her. "Mother?"

"He's a gentleman, and a friend, Preston, but the two don't go together."

"What about Father? Do you not love him anymore?"

Mother sighed, ushering them out of the schoolhouse before locking the door.

"It's nothing to do with that, darling. I'm not being courted by anyone. Do you think I've got the time to do that, even if I wanted to?"

Preston pouted, clearly not happy.

"I don't want anyone else to become our father," he sulked. "I want ours back."

"I know you do, and you don't have to worry about anything. I'm not looking to remarry, not with…" Mother paused and glanced at Florrie. "Not with everything going on right now. Even then, I've got you two to think about. That's more important than anything else."

Florrie knew that much, but she had seen the way the grocer talked to Mother whenever they went in there. He clearly had a fancy for her. A widower himself, he went out of his way to help them whenever he could. He was a decent enough person, and

Florrie liked him, but she didn't think she would be able to manage having someone else to call 'Father'. It would feel like hers had been erased.

Even after everything that had happened, he was still their parent, and Florrie loved him despite what he'd done.

Although she wanted to ask him why. If they were in poverty and struggling as they were, why would he do what he did? Florrie couldn't understand that.

She could only hope it stayed where it was. Their family had enough problems to worry about.

It was a pleasant walk back home. It was near the end of spring and moving into summer, so the days were warmer and there was more vibrant colour around. Even in the middle of Manchester, there was still plenty to see. Those who had the money wore more colourful gowns, jewellery flashing as they walked by, barely giving them a glance. With their tattered clothing needing a wash, those who were of a higher social standing were never going to look at them properly.

The obscurity and anonymity did help, Florrie surmised. There were times when she didn't want to be bothered, and people gave her a wide berth. But it still felt annoying. It shouldn't matter if she didn't have any money. Why couldn't everyone be treated the same?

Nothing to do with her. There was a hierarchy, and she didn't want to deal with getting that into people's heads that they were just like them.

It was gorgeous weather as they passed by the park and entered the grocers for the items Mr Prestwick had for them. He blushed as he handed Mother the bag, and Florrie had to fight back a smile. It was strange, but also sweet, to see a grown man blush. But Preston glared at him and kept glaring until they left. Mother shook her head at her youngest.

"You don't need to be so rude, Preston," she admonished softly. "He's just being kind and helping us out."

"But I don't want him to, Mother," Preston protested.

"Then how are we going to cope without help?"

"We'll think of something."

Mother sighed and continued one, Florrie falling into step with her brother.

"She's not well," she murmured. "Can't you stop being such a brat when she's sick?"

Preston rolled his eyes.

"She's always sick. So what?"

There was no point in arguing, so Florrie fell silent. She knew it would end up with them shouting at each other, and Mother didn't need that.

They reached their home, which was a two-room flat on the ground floor for a house that had been made into three separate homes. Florrie liked it because it had a huge window that looked out into the street and to the park opposite. She spent many hours sitting on the windowsill reading a book and occasionally looking outside. It was soothing.

But there was nothing soothing about the woman standing at the door, dressed in a smart dark green gown with a matching coat and hat, her dark hair pinned up and away from her swan-like neck. She was a handsome figure, but Florrie felt a shiver down her spine when she saw the woman.

Why was she here now? Why couldn't they just be left alone?

Mother groaned and adjusted her hold on the bag.

"I'm sorry, darlings. I've got to talk to her."

"Why is she here again?" Preston glowered at the woman as they approached. "We gave her money last week."

"Because she's still getting her money back, Preston. We can't tell her to go away."

"I wish we could."

Florrie felt the same way. Isadore Credge was a nasty piece of work. She didn't know what the woman really did for a living, but she gave money out and expected it back with a bit of interest. Father had gotten a loan from her, according to Mother, and now she had to carry the debt because he was dead.

Florrie didn't understand it. If the debt was his, surely it died when he did. This just screamed of someone being greedy.

Isadore turned and gave them a mirthless smile as she saw them approach.

"Mrs Walsh," she greeted Mother.

"Miss Credge."

"It's Isadore, you should know that by now."

Mother didn't respond to that, fishing into her pocket as Isadore eyed the groceries in the other woman's arms.

"I hope you've got some left over for me, given you've been getting food for yourself."

"Don't worry, it's all there for you." Mother brought out an envelope and held it out. "There are my week's wages. You take what is yours and give me back the rest."

"Of course."

Florrie wished her mother wasn't so trusting with that. It would be easy for Isadore to skim more of the wages, so they were left with practically nothing. But this time, once the woman had taken what she was owed, she gave it back to Mother.

"That wasn't so hard, was it?"

"Why don't you go away and leave us alone?" Preston asked loudly. "We don't want you here."

"Preston!" Florrie hissed, but Isadore had turned her attention to him. Her eyes glittered.

"I don't want to be here, either, young man, but if your father leaves a debt unpaid, I've got to get my money back somehow."

"So, you take it from a dead man's family," Preston hissed. "How awful can you be?"

"Preston, stop it," Mother warned. "Isadore has other things to do, so we mustn't keep her waiting."

Isadore adjusted her hat, putting the envelope into the reticule she was carrying, closing it with a snap.

"I'll be here same time next week, Mrs Walsh. Don't forget."

"I'm hardly to forget your…visit, Isadore," Mother replied.

The other woman's mouth twitched, and then she walked away. Florrie watched her go, shocked at how elegant and refined Isadore Credge looked and yet she was one of the most horrible people they had ever encountered. Taking money from them and not caring that they were practically destitute. It was making Mother sick.

If they carried on like this, they would end up in the workhouse and they would never be able to get out.

That wasn't going to happen, though. Florrie would make sure that it wouldn't.

CHAPTER 1

Florrie was exhausted as she headed home. Her fingers hurt, and they were stinging from the cold, but it wasn't as bad as she thought it would be. Maybe she was just getting used to it.

At least she would be bringing a decent pay packet home. With her income as well, they were able to use Mother's wages to pay off the unscrupulous money lender Credge and live on Florrie's. It was surprising how well a seamstress was paid despite her age.

It made things a little better at home, although it had taken some time for Mother to agree to it. She hadn't wanted her daughter to throw away her education and start working, but Florrie pointed out that there were plenty of children at her age leaving school and starting work. At twelve, she was more than old enough, and they desperately needed the money, especially with the weather turning cold. How were they going to keep warm during the winter if they didn't have enough money to buy what they needed for a fire?

Mother had eventually relented, and it was at the end of the school year that Florrie started working. She knew Mrs

Hampton as a neighbour who ran a flourishing business, mending clothes for anyone from the most poverty-stricken people to the upper classes. Her name was well-known in the area, and Florrie hoped that she would give her some work or even recommend her for somewhere else.

Thankfully, Mrs Hampton had taken her on, and Florrie was working hard to show that her judgement wasn't misplaced. And it was working because she was getting bigger and more important projects. It was a little startling and it raised a few eyebrows with some people when they heard Mrs Hampton putting a lot of responsibility on a twelve-year-old's shoulders, but Florrie kept her head down and did as she was told.

It worked for her. She certainly needed to do it, otherwise they would have nothing.

"Make sure you have a rest this weekend, Florrie," Mrs Hampton had said before Florrie left her shop for the day. "You're young, and you need to rest yourself. I don't want you getting sick because you're over working."

"I'm fine, Mrs Hampton," Florrie had quickly reassured her. "You don't need to worry about me."

"But I do, dear. You've lost your father, and your mother is always unwell. I'm surprised your family hasn't collapsed already."

Florrie had lifted her chin defiantly.

"That's because we're strong, ma'am. We can weather any storm."

Mrs Hampton sighed.

"I know you and your mother can. You're both very tough. But I wish I could say the same about your brother. He's very… precocious."

Florrie had kept to herself about that, but she could see the woman's point. Preston had been angry and rebellious since their father was killed, but it had been getting worse in recent months. He was lashing out at them, calling Mother names that made her look like she was going to cry, and then he was causing trouble at school. Not just in Mother's lessons but others as well. The teachers had given him plenty of canings and it was a wonder that he could move at all. Florrie half-expected him to be expelled at some point.

But they needed him to stay in school. While he was old enough to work, Mother was adamant about Preston staying in school as long as he could. She wanted to be sure he had enough of an education, and it would be beneficial once he was working. However, from the way Preston was behaving, he seemed to be thinking otherwise. He was sullen and angry, saying that he didn't want to go to school, but whenever Florrie asked what he would do instead he wouldn't answer.

That was worrisome. Florrie hoped he would snap out of it one day. He was going to get into further trouble if he carried on, and it was upsetting Mother. Her health was worse in the winter, and she didn't need the stress over it all.

Florrie wanted to smack him until he saw sense, but that wouldn't do anything. Preston was just angry, and that wasn't going to ease off because she hit him.

It was icy cold now and the light was fading quickly as Florrie reached the park. Normally, she would go around the outside and follow the railings until she reached home, but this time she decided to go through it. Her home was on the other side, so it wouldn't be much of a problem. It was quicker, too.

However, mother had always told her that she should never go through the park. It was far too dangerous, and she was going to end up getting attacked and something would be stolen from her. She also talked about children being kidnapped and taken away for other activities. Florrie had asked about that, but she didn't get a response about it, just that it was bad.

She had an imagination, and she could figure it out on her own. What she did think up made her shiver.

But the cold weather was making her shiver even more. Florrie's coat was getting thin, and it wasn't ideal for the winter. She wanted to get back before her fingers froze even more than they were. They were beginning to sting.

Shoving her hands into her pockets, she pushed the gate open with her shoulder and stepped into the park. With the light fading, it was making all the shadows lengthen, and it was a little murky. Someone had come through a while ago and lit up the gas lamps that lined the path, so at least she had some light, but it just made the shadows around it look darker.

If she was quick, nobody would bother her.

Her heart racing and thinking of the warm fire back home, Florrie half-walked, half-ran through the park. She didn't see anyone, which was a relief. She was looking forward to getting inside and curling up with her mother in front of the fire. It was the warmest spot of the house, to the point the three of them would sleep there at night. Mother kept coughing, but at least she wasn't shivering.

Florrie's heart ached for her. She hated that her mother was in this position. If only there was something they could do for her, but a visit from a doctor would cost money, and it would be frequent as well. They couldn't afford it.

Mother was strong, but her health wasn't good. Florrie was scared that it wouldn't last much longer. No matter how much she tried to hide it, one thing was painfully obvious to Florrie and Preston.

Their mother wasn't getting any better.

As Florrie left the park, closing the gate behind her as she let out a huge sigh of relief, she was startled by a voice behind her.

"I thought you were supposed to keep away from the park, Florrie. I'm sure I've heard your mother tell you that before."

Florrie spun around, her heart in her mouth. Then she saw Isadore Credge. She was standing beside a handsome-looking carriage, completely black from the horse to the wheels. A driver sat up front, holding onto the reins with a blank expression, staring straight ahead.

Credge was the only one with any sort of colour, now wearing a dark red dress with matching hat and a thick coat that looked very warm and comfortable. She was rosy-cheeked, showing how warm she was. It was as if the weather didn't bother her at all.

Florrie glared at her.

"What Mother and I discuss is none of your business," she snapped.

Credge arched an eyebrow at her.

"Do you normally speak with such rudeness towards grownups?" she asked.

"Do you steal money from people who've barely got any in the first place?" Florrie shot back.

"I'm owed this money from your father…"

"And he's dead now, so you should wipe the slate clean and consider it a loss you're never going to get back. Not go after his family because they're still alive." Florrie knew she shouldn't be answering back to the woman, but the last couple of years having to see her belittle and humiliate Mother were getting too much. "Why can't you just leave us alone?"

Credge gave her a curious look and walked towards her. Florrie wanted to back away and put some distance between them, but her feet were rooted to the spot. She couldn't move if she wanted to. Credge looked her up and down and sniffed, towering over her.

"You really should learn not to talk back about things you don't understand. That's not a good idea."

"I know enough to know that you're tormenting a widow with her husband's debt," Florrie answered. She didn't know where she was getting the courage for this. "You think we want to be in this position. Father did something wrong, yes, but why are we being blamed for his wrongdoings? Why not let his debts die with him? Passing them onto his family is just ridiculous."

"You think I shouldn't get my money back even after someone dies?"

"No."

Credge's expression suggested she wasn't sure whether to be angry at being talked back to or curious about Florrie's pluck. She sighed and shook her head.

"You're young, Florrie. How old are you?"

"Twelve."

"Then you don't truly understand the ins and outs of how things work in the adult world. That goes with debts as well. You'll just end up with a lot of problems on your shoulders, and you're too young for that."

Florrie snorted, hands on her hips. The cold wind whipped around them, but she barely noticed it now.

"Too young? You do realize that I must work myself now to help? I must make sure we're not left with nothing when you steal Mother's wages."

"I wouldn't call it stealing…"

"I would. You're horrible to treat us like this. We don't deserve it, and you should leave us alone." Florrie lifted her chin as she glared at the woman. "It's been almost two years since Father died, and you started coming to us to demand payment. Surely, we've paid off the debt by now. Even with the interest you likely tacked on, we must've paid it all back now."

"That's between your mother…"

"Tell me how much Father owed you, and how much interest you put on it," Florrie challenged. "I know how much Mother gets paid every week, so I'll be able to tell if we've paid it off. If not, you're stealing from us."

The flush on her cheeks was getting darker, and Credge's eyes narrowed. She leaned in, and Florrie had to stop herself from pulling back. This woman was scarier than she anticipated. She could feel herself shivering and it had nothing to do with the cold.

Florrie wasn't about to back down.

"You don't need to worry about any of that because it doesn't concern you." The woman's eyes glittered dangerously before she straightened up. "Anyway, you know your mother loves you, right? She's been devastated at the fact her husband died doing something stupid, and I know she's not happy about your brother's...attitude. It would be a shame if something happened to you, too, wouldn't it? That would certainly break her heart."

Florrie's heart almost stopped at that. She wasn't naive enough to know what she meant by that.

"Are you threatening me?"

"Of course not. I wouldn't threaten a child. I'm just warning you that you shouldn't be concerned about things that don't concern you."

Florrie snorted.

"Given that you're targeting Mother and stealing from her, I think it does concern me. Someone must tell you when to go away."

"And it's not going to be a little girl who doesn't know her place." Credge turned away. "It's been an...enlightening conversation, Florrie, but I must go. I've got more important things to worry about than pacifying a little girl."

Florrie wanted to argue that she wasn't a little girl anymore, but she was glad that Credge had decided to leave. She felt as if her skin was crawling because of the woman's presence. She watched as Credge got into her carriage and shut the door with a resounding bang. A moment later, the carriage started moving, and Florrie caught sight of the woman inside as she passed, scowling darkly.

She had angered the woman. But, at this point, Florrie didn't care. She was more worried about her mother. If Credge was here, she had likely just come by to get her money.

Hurrying inside, she found Mother sitting by the fire with a blanket wrapped around her shoulders.

"Mother?" Florrie approached her. "Are you all right?"

"Florrie?"

"I'm here." She sat beside her. "What happened? Credge was here, wasn't she?"

Mother nodded, staring at the flames as they danced in the hearth.

"She took what we owe her this week, but then she started talking about taking more to pay the debt off sooner. Now that you're working…"

"What?" Florrie gasped. "She can't do that! She's been getting more from taking all your wages for months! She's not getting at mine!"

"I told her that would be ridiculous, but she's having a think about it. Something about the sooner we pay the debt off, the sooner we can make her go away." Mother swallowed. Her voice sounded raspy. "I don't think we're ever going to get her away from us. She's never leaving."

Florrie felt sick at the knowledge that her mother was going through this. It was clear she wasn't well, but she was dragging herself to school for work every day regardless. She didn't have any energy beyond that, and then she was getting walked all over by Credge.

"We can tell her to stop," she suggested. "We must've paid off the debt by now. Isn't there a way to find out…"

"I've mentioned that to her before, but Credge says she has her records, and they say we're nowhere near even paying off a quarter." Mother snorted at that. "I don't believe it at all, but this is someone who doesn't care about anything except getting more money. I can hardly believe your father borrowed as much money as he did, especially when he had no way of paying it back so quickly."

"We have to find out somehow," Florrie insisted.

"You let me worry about that." Mother looked around the room. "Has Preston not come back yet? He said he was going out to play with friends, and now it's getting dark."

"No, he's not back. Do you want me to go and find him?"

Mother shook her head.

"Best not. He'll return eventually. I just told him to return at dusk. Hopefully, he'll listen to me."

Florrie hoped so, too, although she doubted it. Knowing Preston, he was doing something to get him into trouble.

CHAPTER 2

1881

"Do you need anything before I head off, darling?" Mother asked as she moved the tailor's dummy to the corner of the room.

"No, Mother, I'm fine." Florrie gave her a smile. "I've got everything sorted, and I've got tasks that I need to do."

"And don't forget to chase up those who haven't paid you yet. You don't want to let them get away with it."

Florrie sighed. That was something she hated doing, but it had to be done.

"I plan to. I'll send out some more letters."

But Mother shook her head.

"I doubt they're going to listen, Florrie. You know what these people are like when they won't pay."

"Maybe I should get paid upfront. Or even half. Mrs Hampton said she did that with those she knew couldn't afford it or gave her the impression they wouldn't pay."

"I think you should do that yourself. But you've got enough custom that you can cope anyway." Mother smiled and hugged her daughter. "I'm so proud of you, Florrie. You're such a strong girl, and I love that you've come into yourself."

Florrie felt her face getting red.

"I don't know what to say to that," she mumbled.

"Just be humble and accept it. That's what I would do." Mother kissed her head. "I hope Preston's doing all right. He said he was going to be out all day, so hopefully he comes back with something."

"He'll likely be back late, knowing him. He did say this employer kept odd hours."

"At least he's earning something. I'm glad about that."

"You need the rest, Mother. We can look after you."

Mother simply smiled and blew her a kiss as she walked towards the door.

"I'm off to the school. See you this evening."

"Bye."

Florrie heard the door open and close, and she got back to sorting out her various orders. There always seemed a lot to do, but she was happy with that. It was better than sitting around twiddling her thumbs.

She was glad that things were turning out well. Just last year, Mrs Hampton had praised her for her work and wished that she could give her more to do. Then it came up that maybe Florrie could try working from home and outsourcing to various places so she would have more work coming in for herself. Florrie had been apprehensive at the thought of doing it on her own - she was only sixteen, so she was still relatively shy - but Mrs Hampton had plenty of contacts and she was more than happy to recommend her.

It had been eight months since she started working out of the second room at their home, and Florrie felt as if things were going well. She worked longer hours, and she was exhausted when she finished, falling asleep almost as soon as she ate her supper, but it felt good having that coming in.

It helped now that Preston was working. Once he turned twelve, he started doing various jobs to bring what he could in. Mother had suggested he become a chimney sweep apprentice but backed down once she found out that the apprentice was the one who went up the actual chimneys to clean them out. She didn't want him doing that.

Besides, he was too big to be going up the flumes, anyway, so he would've gotten stuck. Florrie didn't want to think about her brother being trapped in a tight space with a fire beneath. That would be terrifying.

Now he seemed to have settled down being an apprentice to a local artist who decorated some of the more affluent houses. It meant long hours and he would come back at random times, but he always brought something back. His cut of the pay seemed to be quite good. For a fourteen-year-old, he was a very resourceful boy.

Florrie hoped that this was him getting better with things. He was still somewhat rebellious, but he had calmed down at home, for want of a better phrase. He was still sullen but given his age that was no surprise. And he did help when he was asked.

Hopefully, he would grow out of it all.

As Florrie finished setting up what she planned to do for the day, she heard someone knocking on the door. Checking in the small mirror that she looked presentable enough, she went to the front door and opened it.

A tall, good-looking young man with reddish-brown hair and freckles across his face stood on the doorstep, his hat at a slight angle on his head. He gave Florrie a smile and took his hat off.

"Good morning. Are you Florrie Walsh?"

"I am."

Florrie realised that she was staring a little too much and tried to concentrate on the conversation.

"Forgive me for bothering you like this. My uncle said he'd sent something of his to you to be mended, and he wanted me to pick it up for him." He gave her an apologetic shrug. "He had to head down to London this morning and only just remembered it."

"I see."

"His name's Augustus Charlton?"

"Oh!" The name was immediately recalled. Florrie smiled and stepped aside. "Of course! Come on in."

"Thank you." He stepped inside and gave her a lopsided smile. "I'm Nolan. Nolan Baxter. Augustus' nephew."

"You've said." Florrie shut the door and beckoned him to follow her. "Come with me. It was your uncle's coat that I was fixing. He'd caught it on the door of his carriage and practically ripped the sleeve off."

"He was very upset with that; I can tell you." Nolan entered the room after her and looked around. "At least he found someone to mend it. He's very busy and forgets things like that, especially when he's focused on his business. My aunt knows Mrs Hampton, who recommended you."

"Yes, that's right. If I recall, Mr Charlton was annoyed that he had to wait a few days."

Nolan chuckled.

"Trust me, he completely forgot about it a couple of hours later. It wasn't until he was heading out to the train that he remembered." Nolan dug into his pocket and withdrew an envelope. "He told my aunt to put the money aside to pay you. I hope it's all there."

Trying not to look too eager, Florrie took the packet and counted the money. She had been hoping this job would come to fruition. From what she knew of Augustus Charlton, he was a wealthy man who had made his business in import and export, both in London and Manchester with a few ports out of Cardiff and Swansea. He had been an imposing man who was impatient as he talked to her about the damage, but underneath she could tell that he was very stressed. She wondered if he knew when to slow down and relax. Probably never.

"It's all there," she said with relief. Then she realised how she sounded and flinched. "Sorry, that came out badly, didn't it?"

"Not really." He peered at her curiously. "I take it you have problems with customers not paying."

"You could say that." Florrie put the envelope into a large biscuit her mother had put aside for her to store the money. "They see someone as young as me and think they can get away with treating me as they do. It's frustrating."

"May I ask how old you are?"

"I'm sixteen."

Nolan blinked and stared at her in surprise.

"Really? I thought you were young, but not…" His face flushed and he fumbled with his words. "I mean, that's not…I'm sure you're very capable…obviously, otherwise Mrs Hampton wouldn't recommend…"

"I know what you mean." Florrie couldn't help but smile at his fluster. "I know my age is something that people question a lot. But I do a good job, and I should get paid for it, shouldn't I?"

"Absolutely. It's not fair to do all that work and then get nothing for it." Nolan sighed. "Some people are just under the impression they're entitled to treat people as they see fit, especially those who are of a particular social standing."

"What do you mean?"

"They have a decent amount of money, but because they're not of a lower class or in poverty, they think they can get away with not spending anything because anyone lower than them are not worth it." Nolan rubbed his fingers together. "Let's just say they're tight-fisted and stingy."

Florrie snorted.

"I've been dealing with that for the last eight months. I know what you mean."

"That level of disrespect is just remarkable. You shouldn't have to put up with it."

"I know, but there's only so much…" Florrie stopped when she heard the front door again. Someone was knocking very loudly. "Excuse me a moment?"

"Do you want me to leave?"

"No, it's fine."

That surprised her. She didn't expect that to happen. Normally, she wanted her clients to leave as soon as they had gotten what they needed, especially the young men. She didn't want to be caught in a position where people would talk. But something about Nolan made Florrie want to let him stay.

"I'll just be a moment."

Aware that he was staring at her, Florrie hurried out and to the front door. A large, broad-shouldered man with a bald head and several rings on his fingers towered overhead, giving her a leer.

"Miss Walsh."

"Mr Bakewell. Have you come for your suit?"

"I have, my dear. Is it ready for me?"

It was, but Florrie needed her last payment before she could give it over. They had an accounts book where people could buy now and pay later, and then it would tally up at the end of the month. But it had been three months since Mr Bakewell had been using her services, and that was three months of no payment. Florrie couldn't allow him to continue.

"I've got the final part to do, Mr Bakewell…"

"What? I thought you said it would be ready by now."

Florrie folded her arms. She didn't want to deal with this man.

"I need money to buy the materials needed, sir. And if you're not paying me to get them…"

"It's on the account. It shouldn't be a problem. And you've got money from other customers coming in, haven't you?"

"They're paying for their items, not yours. I'm sorry, Mr Bakewell, but I can't continue until you've paid me for everything."

Mr Bakewell didn't look happy about that at all.

"You're expecting me to pay you?"

"Even those putting it on the account pay at the end of the month, and it's been three. Am I going to see any money at all? Because you won't have a suit ready if you don't pay me."

He leaned in, and Florrie did her best not to pull back. He was an intimidating man, someone who swept in and carried on as if he was the one in charge, and he left no room for argument. Florrie was tired of it, and she wasn't going to let it happen anymore.

"Are you talking back to me, girl?" Mr Bakewell's voice lowered to a dangerous tone. "You're a child. You shouldn't be telling me what to do."

"You're using my services as a seamstress. Surely, you should recognise that I must be paid, no matter how old I am." Florrie could feel herself wavering, but she wasn't about to back down. "If you spoke to Mrs Hampton about me, you should know that."

"You'll get your money. Just when I feel like it."

"What's that supposed to mean?"

Mr Bakewell smirked at her and grasped her chin, his fingers pinching.

"Although maybe we can come to an arrangement."

"What?"

"You're a pretty girl. You'd get more money plying your trade in another way. I can help you with that."

Florrie's stomach churned. He wasn't thinking of…

"That's disgusting." She pushed his hand away. "Pay me to finish your suit, in full, or I'm not doing anything more with it."

"But I need this suit next week!"

"Then you know what to do."

His eyes blazed, and he stepped towards her, making Florrie back up.

"Why, you..."

"Is something the matter?"

Florrie gasped. She had forgotten about Nolan. Now he was walking towards them with a slow stride, his gaze focused on Mr Bakewell. Florrie had never felt so relieved to see someone.

"I don't believe we've been introduced?" Nolan's tone was level as he held out a hand. "Nolan Baxter. I'm Augustus Charlton's nephew."

Mr Bakewell blinked, and then his eyes widened.

"Augustus Charlton?" Mr Bakewell's expression shifted. "You mean..."

"If I recall, you and my uncle are in business together, aren't you? Something about him buying a lot of stock from you over the last couple of years." Nolan raised his eyebrows. "I believe that's something to do with your current wealth. He likes to buy the good things, and he knows when it's good. You can't mess him around as he can spot a fraud for miles."

"Well..."

"He's spoken about you in passing when I've been in his presence, you see. So, I'm guessing from the description he gave of you..." He looked the bigger man up and down. "That you're the Angus Bakewell he's talking about?"

"I...I am Angus Bakewell," Mr Bakewell spluttered.

Florrie wondered what was going on. She knew that Augustus Charlton was a prominent man in Manchester, but she hadn't expected Nolan to know his contacts. She stared at him, but Nolan was focused on her visitor.

"If my uncle is paying you well, then you can afford to pay Miss Walsh what she's owed for making you a new suit, can't you?" Nolan looked him up and down. "Unless you've been using your money for other means, and that means you can top Miss Walsh off because it doesn't matter what she does, does it?"

Mr Bakewell's face had turned pale.

"Well, I...I mean..."

"You're being disrespectful towards Miss Walsh by not paying her. She is in the right to not complete the order if you haven't paid her." Nolan arched an eyebrow. "I presume you don't want the suit as you can't pay for it."

"I do want it!" the other man protested, his face now splotchy with red and white. "I'm in need of a new one for next week when..."

"Save it. If you are in need, you can pay for it. So how about you do that right now with Miss Walsh? Then she can have it ready for you."

Mr Bakewell looked as if he was going to faint. But he nodded stiffly and got out his money bag with shaking fingers.

"I think we should do this inside, don't you?" Nolan stepped aside. "We can balance out the books properly in here. Miss Walsh, if you will go and find out how much Mr Bakewell owes you, then we'll go from there."

Just a few minutes later, Mr Bakewell had paid, and Nolan had arranged for him to get one of his servants to pick up the suit so he didn't have to darken Florrie's doorstep again. She felt like she was in a dream. What had happened there?

She stared at Nolan as he came back into the room after showing Mr Bakewell out.

"Thank you."

"It's not a problem." Nolan gave her a sheepish smile. "I wasn't anticipating being that way, but when I heard Mr Bakewell's voice and how he was speaking to you..."

"So, you really know of him?"

"Uncle Augustus has been grumbling about him. Good quality items, good at talking up a good storm, but apparently has a bad gambling habit."

Florrie stiffened.

"Really?"

"He prefers to bet on the horses more than anything else. That's what gets him into trouble." Nolan peered at her. "I'm sorry if I trod on your toes. I didn't mean to get in the way…"

"No, it's fine." She managed a smile. "I was grateful. I needed that help more than anything. Especially when he started talking about how I could make money in other ways."

Nolan scowled.

"Men like that don't deserve to be around women at all. I don't know how he's been able to stay married as long as he has."

"I'm surprised he was able to find a wife with that attitude."

"Same here. Maybe there's a knack for drawing a woman in. I don't know." He cleared his throat. "Anyway, do you have my uncle's coat? And let me know how much we owe you."

"Of course."

Florrie knew that she couldn't stay talking to him for much longer, but she wished that she could. She really wanted to see what he was like, to talk to him more. There was something about him that drew her attention.

It was a shame it was only going to be a parting gesture, and they'd likely not see each other again.

CHAPTER 3

1882

Mother started coughing harder, which made Florrie flinch. She hurried over and stroked the woman's head as she writhed on the thin mattress.

"Try not to cough so much, Mother," she whispered. "You need to save your strength."

"Strength..." Mother murmured, her eyes half-open. Florrie wasn't even sure that she was paying attention. She was still burning up, and it wasn't going down.

The fever had been there since just before Christmas, and it wasn't going anywhere. Florrie was so scared that she had barely been able to do anything else, sitting by her mother's bedside as she worked. It was the only way she could be comfortable knowing her mother was still there.

But it had been three weeks, and there was no sign of the fever abating. Florrie had been desperate to go for a doctor, but with Credge taking their money as she did, they couldn't afford it, even with Florrie's own wages. She had tried going around looking for someone to help, but she was turned away each time.

Mrs Hampton had offered to pay for her own doctor to look at Mother, but the doctor himself had refused, saying that he wasn't dirtying his hands with grubby poverty brats.

Florrie had never felt as helpless as that.

A sound at the front door drew her attention, and she straightened up, glancing at the clock. It was after six. Was that Preston coming in from work? She needed his help right now; her brother had been spending more time out of the house. He said it was working, but Florrie had a feeling, deep down, that something else was going on.

The door opened and Preston came in. Florrie was shocked at the sight of him. He had a black eye and a bruise on his cheek, which made the side of his face look swollen. His lip was split, and from the dried blood around his nose he'd had a nosebleed as well.

"Preston!" She hurried to him. "What happened to you?"

"It's nothing."

"What do you mean, it's nothing? You've been attacked." Florrie touched his cheek, and her brother flinched. "What happened?"

"Nothing for you to be concerned with, Florrie," he muttered. He pushed her hand away and went to Mother. "How is she?"

"Not good. She's barely conscious, and I don't think she can hear me."

Preston stood over his mother for a while, simply staring down at the mostly still woman. Florrie's heart broke watching him. Despite everything he did, and how he treated them, it was clear that Preston loved Mother. He brought back all his money for her, and Florrie was grateful for that. It was enough to keep their heads just above water, which is what they needed.

If only they could stop paying back their father's debt. It had been seven years. Even with the interest, they should've paid it all off by now. Florrie was still under the impression that Credge was stealing money and making sure they had nothing. The woman was greedy. She also liked being in control. Every time Florrie saw her, there always seemed to be a smugness about her, and she didn't like it.

If only she could leave them alone.

"Anyway, I've got some money for us," Preston said.

"What?"

"I've got some pay today." He dug into his pocket and withdrew some coins. "Do you think that could be enough to afford a doctor?"

Florrie counted the money in his palm and made a quick calculation in their head. She nodded.

"It should be. You know where the nearest doctor is, don't you?"

"Of course. Three streets over in a white house."

"Go right now. Tell him to come immediately." Florrie gestured at his face. "See if he can look at you once he's checked how Mother is."

Preston rolled his eyes.

"It's just a bit of a scratch, Florrie. You don't need to worry about me."

"But I do! What if you'd been attacked and mugged on the way home?"

"It was just a fight with an acquaintance that got out of hand, so you needn't worry." Preston rubbed his chest with a grimace. "The other guy looks worse off."

"That's not something to jest about, Preston! You could've been killed!"

"But I wasn't, and I'm fine. I'll deal with my own injuries later." Her brother gestured at Mother. "She's more important right now. God only knows how she's held on for this long. You know it's bad when she can't get up to go to work."

Florrie knew about that. Mother was on the cusp of losing her job because she had been off for so long. It was unfair, and Florrie had argued that it wasn't right, but there wasn't much she could do about it. She nodded.

"All right. But quickly. Mother needs this treatment yesterday."

"I will." Preston hesitated, now looking nervous. "She's going to be all right, isn't she?"

Florrie managed a smile at him.

"Of course. You don't need to worry about it."

The reality was, she thought sadly as she saw Preston out of the house, she didn't know. Mother's health had been poor all their lives, but she had been able to get up and soldier on. She was tough despite everything, but when she started saying she couldn't get out of bed that was cause of concern.

Her body had given up on her. She had worked so hard that she was unable to move, and now it looked like she was dying.

That couldn't happen. Florrie knew she and Preston needed her more than anything. They couldn't cope without her. Florrie didn't think she knew how to do anything without Mother's guidance. It was very scary.

Just as Preston disappeared around the corner at a sprint, somehow keeping upright with the ice and snow on the ground, a carriage came down the road and pulled up outside the house. Florrie didn't need to see who was inside to know who was visiting; she had seen it too many times.

She folded her arms and glared at Isadore Credge as she climbed out, adjusting her thick fur coat around her. Why did that woman always dress immaculately? It was like she was going to dinner or to the theatre, not collecting money from people who couldn't pay.

Not compared to Florrie, who was standing in the winter evening with no coat on, the wind whipping around her and causing her to keep brushing her hair out of her eyes.

"Don't you ever get tired of this, Credge?" she demanded.

The older woman blinked in surprise.

"I beg your pardon?"

"You've been harassing my family for coming up to seven years now, and you're still demanding money. Surely, you've taken everything you can get out of us by now. Aren't you bored and planning to move onto another target?"

"I'm afraid you're mistaken." Credge approached her slowly, her heels clipping on the slabs. Even with Florrie having grown a lot, she was still shorter than Credge. "I've still got a lot of debt to collect. Your father borrowed quite a lot. I thought he was going to use it to help his family get out of poverty, or to put some aside so your mother would be able to afford a doctor, but to hear he lost it while gambling…"

"As I've said time and again, that's nothing to do with Mother, Preston, and I," Florrie shot back. "You're just stealing our money now. It's getting ridiculous."

"Have you gone to the police about it?" Credge challenged. "Told them that you're being harassed by someone?"

Florrie snorted.

"You think we haven't tried? Of course we have! But they said it was nothing to do with them."

Credge sniggered.

"They're not going to listen to a family who are on the poverty line. They only care about those who have money. You know I could have them arrest you and your family for not paying your debts, should you refuse, and you could end up in debtor's prison."

"They don't send children to debtor's prison."

"Do you want to put yourself in a position to find out?" Credge looked past her towards the house. "Anyway, I'm here to talk to Joanna. Is she in?"

"She's very sick at the moment."

"And that's my problem…?"

Florrie bared her teeth at her. How could this woman be so callous?

"She's sick, as in she's barely able to get up. We can't have a coherent conversation with her, so the chances of you getting any answer out of her that isn't forced is impossible."

"Do you not trust me to just check up on an old friend?"

"Old friend?" Florrie barked out a laugh. "That's a laugh! You've never been a friend to us, and I wouldn't put it past you to threaten Mother further when she's in no fit state to deal with you. You've taken enough of our money so far, so why can't you just go away and leave us alone?"

"And make your debt even worse than it already is?"

"I bet there's no debt anymore. Not after all this time. You've had enough money off us, Credge, so why don't you go away and leave us alone? Find someone else to bully."

Credge's eyes flashed, and she looked Florrie up and down.

"You do know that even if you scream and shout at me, this debt isn't going to go away? It's always going to be there."

"We've paid it off. You're just being greedy at this point because you know Mother can't fight back."

She tilted her head to one side as she regarded Florrie.

"You were never told how much it was, were you?"

"What's that got to do with it?"

"I think you should talk to your mother. She has a contract about it somewhere. Find out just how much you still owe. I think you'll be surprised." Patting her hair, Credge sighed. "As it is, given the situation, I'll come back next week, but it had better be this week's and next week's payment."

"What?"

"I can always go to the police and say you defaulted, if you want. But I'm sure you don't want that to happen." Giving her a smile that didn't reach her eyes, Credge turned away. "Give my regards to your mother. I hope she gets better soon. She needs to, after all."

Florrie stared after her as Credge got back into her carriage and left. She couldn't believe the gall of the woman. Who did she think she was?

She could only hope that Preston got back quickly with the doctor, and then they could see what they could do to make Mother better.

CHAPTER 4

Florrie couldn't believe they were having to do this. It was like a nightmare, and she kept pinching herself in the hopes that they would wake up from it. But it wasn't happening. Mother was dead, and she and Preston were in a dire situation.

Credge thought she could do whatever she wanted. Florrie had believed long ago that the debt wasn't as big as claimed. She had learned a couple of things from some of her clients, who said it was best to get things in writing so nobody would be able to complain about the debt or how much they were paying back. It was only fair to everyone that it was in writing. Naturally, Florrie assumed Father had done the same, but when she demanded to see the paperwork, Credge refused and told her that it wasn't any of her business.

How was it not her business now Florrie and Preston were the ones who had to pay back the debt? Surely, they should be allowed to find out the exact details. But Credge didn't seem to think the same way; she just said she was getting her debt back.

Preston declared that the woman was greedy and didn't care about anyone. Florrie was inclined to agree.

She stood in the single room she now shared with Preston and looked around. It was small, barely enough for somewhere to sleep and a place to cook their food. Even the mattress was thinner than their old one, and that mattress was several years old. But it was all they could afford, the cheapest tenement they could find in Manchester.

The only saving grace was the view from the window. They were on the top floor, right under the roof, and they had an ideal view of the river. Barges would go back and forth, and it looked gorgeous. Even in her low state, Florrie could appreciate that. It was probably the only good thing about their new home.

At least nobody had questioned that they should be going to the workhouse. Given their ages, they were too old for the orphanage, so they would've been taken straight to the workhouse again. If someone had questioned it, they might've had a few problems, but neither sibling was willing to back down. They weren't going to the workhouse.

It wouldn't matter if they were in there or out on the streets; Credge would still want her money.

Preston wanted to tell the authorities about it. He was also certain of her stealing, but Florrie had a feeling they wouldn't be believed. If you didn't have money, the police didn't want to know. She hated how it worked, but there wasn't much they could do about it.

"I've managed to get a job."

Florrie turned. Preston had entered the room, a surly expression on his face, but she could see how bloodshot his eyes were from crying. Not that her little brother would admit it, of course.

"That was quick," she remarked. "We only moved in an hour ago."

"There are several merchants along the canal, and they're looking for people to work on the barges, taking them back and forth with their supplies." Preston shrugged. "I just asked a few if they needed odd jobs doing, and they said I could do a bit for them."

"So you might be on a boat for days at a time?"

"Possibly. The money isn't too bad, and it's better than nothing."

Florrie had to concede that, but she was still worried. Preston was only fourteen, and he might claim he knew the way of the world, but he would still be out of his depth. Aside from an obvious point as well, which made her worry even more.

"You can't swim," she pointed out.

Preston rolled his eyes as he joined her at the window.

"It's something. We can't knock it back because I can't swim. I'm sure most of the men working on the boats can't either."

"Even so..."

"And the man I spoke to knows about you needing a job as well, and apparently his wife is a seamstress. She gets a lot of work in and has been looking for others to come and help her. He's going to speak to her about bringing you in."

Florrie was glad she might have something, although she was sad that she wouldn't be able to do her own business from their room. While it had been tough, at least she got to keep all the pay instead of giving her employer a cut. But she had to admit to this, she couldn't do much in the room they were in, not without getting rid of something.

At least she got a job she liked doing, so that was better than nothing. And Florrie knew how much she got paid. A chunk of her pay packet was going to Credge, so she needed to plan carefully.

"I hate this," Preston muttered, folding his arms and scowling out at the river docks. "Mother should still be alive. If we could afford a doctor in time, or if we could've afforded one without paying back that witch..."

"There's nothing we can do about it now, Preston. We just must make do with what we've got."

"And Credge gets to steal money from children? That's essentially what she's doing, isn't it?"

Florrie couldn't argue with that. But what could they do? They were not grown, so they were easier to bully. Even if they fought back, Credge would still have the upper hand.

"I wish we could do something about that woman," Preston growled.

Florrie frowned at him.

"Like what?"

"I don't know. But I've had a lot of horrible thoughts about her, most of them that would get me hanged if I did them."

How did she respond to something like that? Preston having dreams about torturing Credge was horrible, but Florrie couldn't scold him for it. She had been having the same thoughts, and they were very graphic. She had never thought her rage would be like that, and she wasn't about to let it take over.

Although it would be very satisfying.

"I wish Mother was here," Preston whispered. "I miss her. I can't believe she's gone now."

"I know. I miss her, too."

Her brother didn't say anything for a moment. Then Florrie realized he was shaking, and a sob escaped from his mouth. He bowed his head, and the shaking got worse. She immediately put her arms around him and hugged him. Preston grabbed onto her with a grip that made Florrie wince, and then he began to cry. He hadn't cried since they realized Mother was dead, bottling it up even during the meagre funeral they had managed to hold for her. Florrie knew that he was trying to be strong, but it was easier said than done. Being strong was hard, even for her. Even now, she could feel her own tears itching her eyes.

She wanted to take away the pain, to make things better for both, but how was she going to do that when they were in this predicament?

It took a while for Preston to calm down, and then Florrie

laid him on the mattress, hoping that he would rest. Preston had barely slept since Mother died, saying that he didn't need it. But soon he was sound asleep, snoring softly. Florrie left him to it, quietly leaving the room and heading outside. The smell from the river wafted past her nose as she stepped out into the street, along with the acrid smoke from the nearby factories, and from the boats chugging back and forth in the river.

That was the downside of living that close. It was going to be disgusting smelling that every day, but Florrie knew there would be no point in arguing about it. They weren't able to do that.

She was looking forward to getting to work, though. Sitting around twiddling her thumbs while they waited for Credge to come by was not going to help. The sooner they got started on their work, the better.

She needed to find the woman who was looking for seamstresses.

It didn't take long before she entered a terraced house by the bridge, entering a living room that seemed to be larger than the only room she and Preston now lived in. A buxom woman with greying dark hair and a red birthmark up the side of her face was sitting by the window, her head down as she sewed the hem of a shirt. She looked up as Florrie came in.

"Mrs. Irons?"

"Yes?" she said in a clipped tone. "Can I help you? I'm afraid I don't have any free appointments today."

"I'm not here for an appointment. Not really, anyway."

"What does that mean?"

Florrie bit her lip, hoping that she wasn't going to get thrown out.

"I was told that you were looking for seamstresses to help you out. I'm looking for work, and I thought you might like…"

Her voice trailed off. Was she saying too much? Florrie felt as if she was tripping over her own feet. Mrs. Irons tilted her head to one side, lowering her sewing.

"You can sew, can you?"

"Yes, ma'am. I've been a seamstress for the last few years."

"I see." She looked Florrie up and down. "You're so young. How old are you?"

"I'm seventeen next month."

"I've not seen you around here before."

Florrie swallowed. She could feel her throat tightening, and it was uncomfortable.

"My brother and I…we just moved here. We're looking for work right now, and we'll take on whatever we can."

"Just the two of you?" Mrs. Irons frowned. "Where are your parents?"

Just saying that they were dead made Florrie unable to speak. She wasn't about to burst into tears in front of a prospective employer. However, from her hesitation the woman seemed to realise what she was holding back, and her expression softened.

"Oh, my dear. I'm sorry. That was rude of me."

"It's fine."

"It's never fine." She gestured at the seat across from her, putting aside her sewing. "Come and sit with me. What's your name, dear?"

"Florence Walsh." Florrie sat down, absently brushing down her skirts. "I'm known as Florrie."

"I'm Annabelle Irons. My husband works here on the river docks, getting everyone organised. His words." Mrs. Irons smiled. "You can imagine how boring it gets down here if you're not part of the river company, but if you find work then you're pretty much set."

"My brother said you were looking for people to help you with your own business?"

The woman nodded and gestured to the pile of clothing, neatly folded, in a basket by her feet.

"I've got so much to do that I'm forgetting that I need to eat and get some sleep. My husband is getting worried about my own health. This is coming from someone who smokes and eats so much I'm surprised his trousers haven't burst already. He can't even swim, and he's been so close to falling into the water many times."

"My brother said he couldn't swim, either."

"Trust me, that's not something anyone is worried about as long as the work gets done. It's a horrible thing to say, but that's how things are. Anyway, I'm pretty much doing work for everyone in the docks, but I'm determined to get it sorted. However, my husband is right, and I need a few people to give me a hand. I will make myself ill if I work like this so much."

"I'm a fast worker," Florrie said eagerly. "I even worked for myself for a few months not too long ago."

"You did?" Mrs. Irons arched an eyebrow. "At your age?"

"We needed the money. Then Mother…"

She stopped, realising what she was about to say. Mrs. Irons seemed to understand what she was saying, though, and gave her an understanding nod.

"I understand what you're saying, darling. It's never easy, and we must figure out ways to survive. You can do whatever you want if you put your mind to it." She paused. "I would appreciate it if you could work fast and work long hours. I'll split whatever money I get between us evenly, if you do the work. Communication is key."

"Of course," Florrie agreed. "And I will do whatever I can."

It was better than nothing, and Florrie hoped from the pile of clothes that they would get quite a bit of money coming in. Then again, she didn't know how Mrs. Irons charged everyone and if she did something for free. That would be tough to manage, but she wasn't the one in charge.

"Why don't you show me how good you are, dear?" Mrs. Irons picked out a dress and handed it over. "The seam is ripped, and the shoulders need letting out. The girl who wears this is growing at an alarming rate, so we want to get as much use out of this dress as we can."

"Of course."

"I've got a sewing basket that you can use." The woman gestured at the basket under the window. "But if you have your own things, that's more than helpful."

"I do," Florrie said quickly. "It's back in my room."

"Run along and get it, dear. Then you can get started. I want to see how good you are."

Florrie didn't need to be told twice. She needed to get on with bringing money in as soon as possible. She didn't get the option to stop, not with Credge breathing down their necks. She might not know where they had moved to, but it wouldn't take much for her to find them.

Florrie could only hope, in her wildest dreams, that the mean woman would forget about them and think that Florrie and Preston had disappeared into the workhouse where she couldn't get hold of them, or left the city completely. Anything to make her go away.

CHAPTER 5

1883

"That's the lot for today, I think," Mrs. Irons declared as she put the final piece of clothing into the basket with a sigh of relief. "I thought we were never going to get finished."

"It did feel like everyone descended on us this past week," Florrie agreed, flexing her sore fingers. "And we'll be back to it tomorrow."

"As normal. But we won't have a backlog of work to do, so that's something." Mrs. Irons smiled at her. "Why don't you take the afternoon off?"

Florrie thought she had misheard. She stared at her employer.

"Take the afternoon off? Are you sure?"

"Why not? We're not going to be doing anything except just sit here and enjoy the nice weather, so why don't you go and have a few hours to yourself? I'm sure you've been working nonstop since I hired you."

She did have a point. Apart from a couple of days here and there, Florrie had been working vigorously to bring the money in. Mrs. Irons, to her credit, was a good employer and she did keep her promise to split the pay evenly between them. She was a kindly person as well, feeling like a grandmother to Florrie, using her patience and cool demeanour whenever she had a few customers who weren't happy or tried to get out of paying. Mrs. Irons didn't have a problem with putting someone in their place.

Florrie hoped she could do that when she was old enough. Even though she was eighteen now, her age was against her and people thought they could take advantage of her. Arguing on Mrs. Irons' behalf when she wasn't around wasn't easy, but slowly she had gotten the respect she deserved. Mrs. Irons had made sure of that, anyway.

"You don't need to worry about anything, dear," the old woman said when Florrie hesitated. "If any work comes in, we can sort it out tomorrow. I'm going to head into the market a few streets away and have a look around. Maybe you can do the same? You've not been there, have you?"

"No. Just too much to do."

"Then why don't you go and explore? You're still young, so you should be able to do it."

Florrie couldn't argue with that. Preston had been to the market a few times to get supplies for whoever he was working for, and he had gushed about how vibrant it was. There had been a wistful note to his voice, and Florrie had needed to be sure that her brother wasn't beginning to steal again. It had turned into something of a compulsion, and Preston still had the temptation. But her brother promised that it wasn't going to happen. That was behind him.

Florrie doubted it, but she wasn't about to argue with him. She just had to trust him.

"By the way," Mrs. Irons said as Florrie headed towards the door. "Has that woman come by?"

That made her heart stop for a moment, and she stared at the woman.

"What?"

"I believe she said her name was Isadore Credge. She was looking for you and your brother. Something about you still owe her." Mrs. Irons frowned. "I didn't tell her where you lived, but I can't guarantee that someone else hasn't pointed her in your direction."

Florrie felt her heart sink. She had decided once she started working for Mrs. Irons that she wasn't going to send money to Credge anymore. She was taking more than they had, and Florrie didn't believe there was a debt. She had sent a letter stating that she wanted to see the records with her father's signature on it saying he would pay off the debt, and if that wasn't produced and looked like a real article, then she wasn't paying. She couldn't afford a solicitor to get that sorted, but she couldn't do that. Although it didn't matter, seeing as Credge didn't know where to send a letter in response. As far as she was concerned, Florrie and Preston had run away, even though they were about thirty minutes away from their former home.

Even though she was earning for herself and her brother, Florrie did feel like she was looking over her shoulder all the time.

"I was hoping I'd never have to deal with that woman again." She rubbed the back of her neck. "She was so adamant about draining us dry."

"Maybe you should consult a solicitor and see if you can get her to back off?" Mrs. Irons suggested. "If you send it down the legal route, then that might help."

"Preston and I barely make enough to do that. And Credge is very clever. She can manipulate something to make it look as if she's the one in the right."

"You can't be like this forever, dear. Running away from someone bullying you. And what she's doing, going after children for a debt, is wrong."

Florrie wanted to point out that she was eighteen now, Preston sixteen, and they were hardly children anymore. But

Mrs. Irons was right: what Credge was doing was wrong, and yet she didn't seem to care about it. She had found someone to give her money regularly, and she was making the most of it. It had been eighteen months since Florrie had sent her anything, so she must've been going mad wondering where the siblings were. It was nothing short of a miracle they had lasted this long without being found.

That was coming to an end now.

"Maybe I should stay home," Florrie suggested. "If Credge is around, going to the market…"

"You cannot let her control your life, Florrie. If you see her coming towards you, just scream and make a fuss. She'll be too embarrassed to approach you with people looking at you two."

Florrie hesitated. She didn't know if she could do that. She wasn't brave enough.

"I don't know…"

"Just scream that she's a child snatcher or something. That would really embarrass her."

"What?"

Mrs. Irons grinned.

"I've done that before when I was your age. Nobody likes people who snatch children off the streets, so they would end up getting bombarded with everyone else. I think it would work even now."

Florrie didn't know about that, but she hoped that it wouldn't come to that.

It was a lovely day as she stepped outside, the warm sun on her face and a gentle breeze wrapping around her. She had gotten used to the smell coming from the river, and how noisy it was at night when she was trying to sleep. While she didn't get paid too badly by Mrs. Irons, she and Preston had to count their pennies every day to make sure they had enough. Preston was working as many odd jobs as he could find, and he was now beginning to have people turn to him if they needed anything done. He was more than happy to help if he was paid, and he worked even longer hours than Florrie. It was a surprise if he ended up coming home at a normal time.

Florrie hoped that he wasn't stealing again. She was too scared about him getting caught and arrested. Preston might promise, but she wasn't sure if she could completely trust him.

She would find out eventually, she was sure.

She made her way through the streets to the market, which Mrs. Irons had been correct about. It was bustling and thriving, so many stalls around and people selling their wares. They seemed to be jovial and happy, and the atmosphere was light and pleasant. Florrie found herself wandering through the streets, looking at the various stalls. She didn't have much money on her after being paid that day, and she wanted to save it for the rent and getting some food later.

But there was nothing wrong with looking. It was fun, and she found herself pouring over the books on a book stall. They were battered and looked to have seen better days, but the variety was big.

If only she could buy herself a book. It would be something to do in the evenings, just curling up by the window and reading as the world chugged by. But Florrie wouldn't be able to afford a book without losing out on something else. There were only so many meals they could miss before their stomachs started hurting, and Florrie had missed too many lately.

Sighing, knowing that she couldn't buy anything before her, she turned away, only to bump into someone coming the other way.

"Oh!"

"I'm sorry, I didn't..." Then the gentleman's voice tailed away. "Miss Walsh?"

Florrie looked up. The man standing before her, almost towering over her, looked very familiar. He was dressed in nice clothes, a hand to shield his face from the sun, sporting a square, clean-shaven jaw and a soft-looking mouth. He knew her, but how did she…?

Then it clicked as a memory shot through her head. The young man who had rescued her from a rude customer, who had given him a dressing down. Florrie's mouth fell open.

"Mr Baxter?"

"I'm flattered you remember me." His cheeks went a little pink as he took off his hat. "It's good to see you again."

"And you. It's been a while."

Florrie couldn't believe she could remember someone from two years ago, and just one interaction. Her heart fluttered as she took him in. He was far more handsome than she recalled.

Why was her mind going to that immediately? She shouldn't even be looking at him in such a way. That was inappropriate.

"I…" She cleared her throat. "How are you? Busy life?"

"You could say that. That's the joy of being over the age of eighteen now." He nodded at the book stall. "Avid book reader, are you?"

"Well…"

How was she going to admit that she didn't have any money? Nolan Baxter would still remember how things were for her in the past, but if she told him things weren't any better, he would be looking at her with pity. She wasn't about to go through that, not when she wanted to keep talking to him.

Even with her heart pounding so hard she felt lightheaded.

"Would you permit me?" Noal asked.

"I beg your pardon?"

"To buy you a book."

Florrie stared at him.

"You would get me a book?"

"Why not? We all need a bit of joy in our lives, and I believe books do that for us." He smiled. "It won't be much, and it will be my way of thanking you."

"Thanking me? But I'm the one who should be thanking you, Mr Baxter. You're the one who helped me with that awful man..."

"It's Nolan, please. And I don't mind at all. There's nothing wrong with getting a gift for someone who helped my uncle out as well as she did."

Florrie thought about denying him, but she knew she would be fighting a losing battle. Especially if it would draw attention to them. Biting her lip, and feeling very uncomfortable, she nodded. Then they spent the next few minutes looking through the books and picking out a few.

Florrie had wanted to stick to just one book, but Nolan said he didn't mind buying a few more. The shopkeeper looked as bemused as Florrie felt, glancing at her whenever Nolan picked up a book to show her. Maybe he thought she wasn't worthy enough to get a book, and there might be an additional payment later.

Florrie felt a little embarrassed thinking about that. But if Nolan was going to show her kindness, she wasn't going to argue, even if it was a little uncomfortable for her.

Finally, they had bought five books, and Nolan now carried them for her as they walked back to the docks. He had been insistent on walking her home, although Florrie wasn't looking forward to him seeing where she lived now. He was aware that her mother had died, and she'd needed to move, but if he knew her poverty situation it would be humiliating. Florrie didn't want him to think any less of her.

She was looking forward to reading the books they had picked out, though. It had been a while since she had curled up with a book, since she'd needed to sell them to pay for Mother's funeral years ago. It had been devastating to part with them, and Florrie wished she could have them back.

It would take time.

"So," Nolan said as they turned onto the path by the river, the water sloshing as the barges went past. "What are you doing now? Are you still a seamstress?"

"I am. I work with someone else. She's very kind to me."

"And your brother? You mentioned something about him."

"He's working on the docks."

Nolan frowned at her.

"And you're getting by, aren't you? I know things were tough for you before, but now..."

"We're fine," Florrie cut him off quickly. "You don't need to worry about that aspect."

"Are you sure? I can help..."

"We can manage things on our own, Nolan. It's fine."

Florrie didn't believe that, but she was not about to accept anything from Nolan Baxter. He looked so handsome, so well-off, that it would feel like he was giving her charity. She couldn't do that. Besides, if Preston found out that she was allowing someone to help them, he would accuse her of something immoral. He was far more suspicious than she was.

"How are things on your end?" Florrie asked. "You're still working for your uncle, aren't you?"

"I was, but things...happened."

"What do you mean?"

Nolan sighed.

"Uncle was the eldest son, and he took over the business from Grandpa. Father also worked in the business, but he wasn't going to take over unless something happened to my uncle." He hesitated. "Then he died about six months ago, and Father took over the business."

"I see." Florrie bit her lip. "I'm so sorry for your loss."

"You don't need to be. It's just something that happens."

"People dying shouldn't be something that simply happens."

Nolan grunted. He was absently swinging the parcel of books in his hand, looking across the river to people on the other side. There was a man and a woman walking together with a maid not too far behind, appearing to be in the throes of courtship. Florrie had noticed them as well. They looked happy, glancing at each other with love evident across the water. She hoped that would happen to her one day, to be courted by someone who loved her dearly.

But that was a far-off dream. She wasn't going to dwell on it.

"Anyway, Father has started laying down the law, so to speak," Nolan went on. "He's being stricter with the workers, and with me as well. We didn't have a good relationship to begin with, but now it's getting worse."

Florrie frowned.

"I thought you were going to inherit the company from your uncle. You said something about that when I last saw you."

"I thought so, too. But apparently Uncle never updated his will. So it went to his brother, my father." Nolan made a face. "Now he's trying to get rid of me. He wants me to work as a merchant seaman."

"What?"

"He says I need to know what genuine hard work is, and I must go out into the real world. In his eyes, that means going to work on a ship in the middle of the ocean, something he's never done. And yet he thinks it's how men are made."

Florrie was shocked. She had wondered about Nolan now and then over the years, but to hear that his predicament was not as she thought was surprising.

"At least you have a roof over your head and family that care about you," she pointed out. "That works out for you that way."

Nolan glanced at her, his expression solemn. Florrie had already told him about Mother dying, which he had expressed condolences for.

"I'm moaning about something I should be grateful for, aren't I?" he said with a grimace.

"A little bit. I understand you don't want to be a seaman, and you want to stay as you are, but at least you have choices."

"You have choices as well, Florrie. Everyone has them."

Florrie didn't agree with that. While she hadn't told Nolan how bad it was for her, he had likely guessed from her attire and how tired she looked. He had been kind enough not to mention it, and he didn't seem to mind spending time with her.

She was going to feel miserable when he walked away from her and never came back.

CHAPTER 6

Much to her surprise, he did come back. After dropping her off at the end of her street, Nolan had asked to see her again. Florrie hadn't expected that at all, but she was more than happy to agree. Although she wasn't sure when her next day off would be, given that she was working all hours she could. But Nolan gave her his address and promised to come once she let him know. They would work something out.

It felt good to have a friend again. Florrie had been feeling a little alone. She had Preston, who was barely around, and Mrs. Irons was kind and friendly - they could talk about anything - but she didn't have friends to spend time with when she wasn't working. It wasn't easy.

Now Nolan was around, and Florrie felt much better about it.

"Where are you heading off to?"

She jumped, spinning away from the small mirror she had propped up on the mantlepiece. Preston had come in, looking thinner and more tired than the last time, she had seen him. He dropped a bag on the floor as he closed the door. Florrie glanced at the bag.

"I hope those were procured honestly," she remarked.

Her brother rolled his eyes and nudged the bag towards the wall with his foot.

"You don't need to worry about any of that. I'm not stealing anymore. I gave you, my word."

Florrie knew that much, but she still worried about Preston and his penchant for taking things that didn't belong to him. They didn't need the police at their door.

"Anyway, you didn't answer my question." He folded his arms. "You're dressed nicely, and you've even done your hair. I thought you were going to work."

"I am."

"But you don't need to dress like you're going out when you're only going ten houses down the street."

Florrie could feel her face getting warm. She bit her lip and tried not to feel awkward. It wasn't any of his business, and yet he was behaving as if he was her father.

"I'm just going to meet a friend afterwards, that's all."

"A friend?" Preston tilted his head to one side. "A male friend. When did you have time to meet a man?"

"I'm not doing anything inappropriate, Preston. I'm just spending time with someone who isn't you."

"Charming. But how do I know that he's going to be a gentleman?"

"Preston…"

"I'm just wanting to be sure that he's not going to hurt you." For a moment, his expression shifted. "It's just us two now. I don't want to lose that."

Florrie understood that, and her heart melted a little. Even with him keeping her at arm's length and barely interacting with her, her little brother still cared. She crossed to him and kissed his cheek, which made him make a face at her.

"Yuck!"

"You're really sweet sometimes, do you know that?"

"Don't say that out loud, whatever you do." Preston wiped his face with his sleeve. "I don't want to ruin my reputation around here."

Florrie laughed.

"Reputation? You should be so lucky. Anyway, I'm heading to work so don't worry about me."

"That's easier said than done." Preston yawned, stretching his arms above his head. "Anyway, don't get into trouble until I've woken up. I've been up all night, and I'm exhausted. I need sleep."

Leaving their single room, Florrie headed out and walked down the street. Summer was turning into autumn, and it was starting to get a little cooler during the day. It was nice, and Florrie found herself feeling lighter. When it was hot, the river docks got very stuffy, and it was stifling. This felt better, allowing her to breathe more easily. Who knew she would get used to the smell of river water and the smoke coming from the various boats going back and forth?

At least she and Preston were still safe. Credge had been seen around the docks asking after them, but Florrie had discovered something about the people who worked there; they were tight-knit and weren't about to give away anyone who lived on the street with them. If the person being asked after was decent and respectful - as both Florrie and Preston were - then they would get the protection from the workers on the river. Florrie had heard from Mr. Irons that Credge had asked around, and then had left in frustration when she realised, she wasn't getting what she wanted.

It felt nice, although Florrie did worry that she would get caught one day.

"You're in a very good mood today," Mrs. Irons remarked as they finished their work for the day. "You've been smiling more, and your humming is really sweet."

"What?" Florrie bit her lip. "Sorry."

"No need to apologise. It was nice to see you in a good mood." The older woman looked amused. "So, who's the lucky man?"

"Man?"

"You've been like this for the last three months, Florrie. I have a feeling it's because a gentleman has come into your life and made things nice for you." Mrs. Irons winked. "I've been like this myself, when I first met my husband. Apparently, it was like I was walking on air."

Florrie could feel her face getting warm as she blushed. Now this was more embarrassing than Preston figuring it out. She busied herself with folding the finished items she had been sewing.

"I've just gotten reacquainted with an old friend, and we're catching up. That's all."

"From the way you're blushing, something more is happening."

"Mrs. Irons!"

The seamstress laughed and reached into the box she used to keep the money, splitting it evenly between the two of them. Putting Florrie's half into an envelope, she handed it over.

"There you go, dear. And are you sure about working longer hours every now and then? You look exhausted, and I don't want to push you more."

"We've gotten busier recently, haven't we?" Florrie shoved the envelope into her pocket. "I don't think we can keep up if just you is just working longer hours. It's only fair that I do my fair share as well."

"You're very kind, my dear, but you're so much younger than me. You should be enjoying your free time."

Florrie couldn't help but smile at this. Mrs. Irons was the kindest employer she'd ever had. She was more concerned about her having fun and making the most of it instead of making her work harder and longer. There was one word you could describe the woman sitting before her: fair.

And she needed the money. Even with Preston's work bringing money in, they still struggled to get the rent together and eat. Their landlord had been genial enough when they first moved in, but then he passed away and gave the properties he owned to his son, who kept raising the rent. Florrie had tried to ensure that the price stayed the same, but it hadn't happened. Not unless she did something sordid for the new landlord, and Florrie wasn't about to lower herself down to that level.

She had to keep up with the rising rent somehow.

Trying not to think about her landlord coming over the next day for his rent money, Florrie left Mrs. Irons house and headed towards the bridge. She and Nolan met there often, Florrie not wanting him to walk her home. Mostly because she was more protected on her street than anywhere else, and because she didn't want to be teased about having a well-dressed gentleman friend. Nolan kept offering, but Florrie wasn't about to do that.

They were friends, nothing romantic. Although whenever she looked at him her heart wouldn't stop racing, her body felt warm, and Florrie found herself wanting to lean into him to savour it more. She wanted to feel his arms around her, to feel like someone wanted her.

Nolan had never given any indication that he wanted anything more, though, and she wasn't about to push it. That would have him walking away, and she would be humiliated.

Sure enough, Nolan was leaning on the bridge when Florrie arrived, staring into the water below with a solemn look on his face. Immediately, she could tell that something was wrong. She joined him, leaning on the parapet beside him.

"Tuppence for your thoughts?"

"Hmm?" He blinked up at her, and Florrie could tell that he had been completely lost in his own head. "Florrie?"

"You hadn't forgotten that you and I were meeting, did you?"

"No, I...I hadn't." He rubbed his eyes and straightened up. "Sorry, I was...thinking about something else."

"That much was obvious." Concerned about his welfare, she

leaned her hip on the parapet and folded her arms. "What's wrong? Has something happened?"

Nolan sighed heavily.

"You could say that. Father is still insisting that I get onto a merchant ship."

"I thought you've been telling him no for months now."

"I have, but he's still not listening. He wants me to sail to India with the next merchant ship he can find."

Florrie's heart stuttered at that. India? Her geography wasn't great, but she knew that India was a country in the middle east, and it was a large place. The British had gone over there, and they were establishing businesses that were growing rapidly. Everyone knew that having business in that country meant things would be ideal for their revenue. And Nolan's father wanted to send him there?

"You've told him no, though, haven't you?" she asked quietly.

"Of course I did!" Nolan looked as if that was a stupid question. "I want to work here, on the shore where the floor stays in one place, and I can escape at the end of the day. But he's refusing to listen to me."

"How can he refuse? It's just madness that he would send you along and he doesn't care about you."

"I don't think he cares about anything except getting what he wants. He's been like that since he was a child, according to my uncle." Nolan spoke with a bitter tone. "I didn't understand it when I was a child, and I still don't. I don't understand the logic of me getting on a ship to make me into a man when he didn't do it himself."

"Maybe he's trying to get rid of you?"

"But why would he do that? We don't get along, but that shouldn't be enough to get rid of me." Then Nolan closed his eyes with a groan. "Unless it's because of what happened last year."

Florrie frowned.

"What happened then?"

"I broke off an engagement."

"What?" She thought she had misheard. "You broke off an engagement?"

He nodded, looking sheepish as he leaned back against the parapet. Now he couldn't look her in the eye, and Florrie could feel the discomfort coming off him.

"It was an arranged thing. Her parents were wealthy, and Father hoped to get the two of us married so he could have them as benefactors for the business. It would make us more prosperous."

"I see."

Florrie could understand marrying another family as a kind of business transaction but knowing that Nolan had been engaged before left her with a nasty taste in her mouth. She tried to push the discomfort away to focus on him.

"I didn't want it. Mostly because it wasn't my choice and because I hated her."

"You hated her?"

"Clarissa was a nasty girl. Only daughter, so she was spoiled immensely by both of her parents. She looked down on other people and treated their servants horribly. When she remarked about having very few friends she could rely on, I did think it was because, even with her wealth and family connections, she wasn't a person others wanted to be around. But Father said she was of marriageable age, and she would be a good wife for me."

"And you disagreed."

Nolan scoffed at that.

"Absolutely. She would ruin the business. All she knows what to do is spend money and be rude. Father said I didn't have an option, and at the time, I thought that was the case. But last Christmas, she and her parents had come to dinner, and Clarissa started talking about how she was supposedly given bad work by a seamstress, and she refused to pay, calling them a variety of names before they agreed to do the alterations again without asking for payment. Apparently, it was something she did regularly, saying something was sub-par and then getting it for nothing."

Florrie arched an eyebrow.

"This is coming from a rich girl who could buy anything."

"If it's to her advantage, she'll make sure she gets to be rude to someone. She looks down on everyone she deems beneath her. Her parents were nodding along as if this was the most normal thing to do. I just..." Nolan paused and glanced at her. "I remembered how you had to deal with that rude customer when I was there, and how he was prepared to steamroll over you. I knew I couldn't sit there and let it continue, and I didn't want to be associated with someone who was like Clarissa. So, in front of our parents, I ended the engagement and stated why."

"I bet that didn't go down well with anyone."

Nolan grunted, running his fingers through his hair.

"Absolutely not. Father was furious, and Mother got faint. Clarissa's parents were shocked that I would do such a thing. They were, at the very least, chastised when I told them they shouldn't allow anyone to be treated badly as it looks like they're awful people who can't be trusted. It didn't matter how much they donated to charity and the like, if they treated others abysmally that was remembered more, and they would be seen as hypocrites. Appearances are important to them."

"And yet they were willing to let their daughter behave as she did," Florrie murmured. "How did she take it?"

"As you would expect. Angry, shocked, upset. She threw a tantrum and stomped her feet when I said I didn't want a childish brat as my wife. She said I wouldn't get anyone better than her, and she was going to make sure everyone knew how horrible I was. Father said that I would regret throwing away a good engagement, especially with her parents refusing to fund the business because of how their daughter had been treated. Nice to

THE ORPHAN'S HOPE IN MANCHESTER

see that their attitude after being scolded was temporary, and it was all about their daughter."

"And now he's trying to send you away?"

"I'm not going. I refuse to go anywhere." He lifted his head and looked at her. "Especially when I've got a reason not to leave England."

Florrie felt a tingling down her spine, and she peered at him. Part of her hoped he was saying she was the reason, but she knew she shouldn't get her hopes up.

"I...what is the reason?"

Nolan smiled and leaned towards her. His kiss was gentle, to the point Florrie wasn't even aware that she had been kissed. He was still smiling when he pulled back.

"Does that give you an indication?" he asked. "Will that tell you something?"

"I...I think so." Florrie touched her mouth. She had never been kissed before, and it felt strange. "I don't know what to say."

"Don't say anything. Just say that you and I can spend as much time as we can together, just the two of us."

Florrie didn't need to question him further on that. It was something she wanted of her own. Even with her longer work hours, and the worries about being found by Credge, she wanted to have something that was all for her and she didn't need to share it with anyone else.

She couldn't remember if she had ever had something - or someone - to call her own before. Mrs. Irons had told her that she needed to have time for herself to do whatever she wanted. Now was her chance.

She smiled and took Nolan's hand.

"I'd like that," she said. "That would be perfect."

CHAPTER 7

884

"What happened to you?"

Florrie winced when she heard Preston's voice. She had hoped to get herself sorted and more presentable before he returned home, but apparently, he decided to come back whenever he wanted. Now her brother was standing in the doorway staring at her in shock.

"It's fine," she assured him. "It doesn't hurt."

"What do you mean, it doesn't hurt?" Preston demanded. "You've got a black eye coming up, your lip is swollen and cut, and one cheek is red."

"Just superficial."

Preston stormed across the room and gently clasped her face in his hands as he inspected her closely. Florrie flinched when his fingers brushed over the bruise on her cheek. It hadn't looked too bad in the mirror, but she knew it would blossom into an impressive black eye in the morning.

"Someone attacked you, didn't they?" Preston's expression was angry. "Was it Credge? Has she found us?"

"No, it...I don't think it was her people."

"Her people…"

"There were four of them as I was coming back from Mrs. Irons' house. They attacked me and took…" It hurt to talk, and Florrie had to slow down a little. "They took my wages. Mrs. Irons had only just given it to me, and they stole it away."

"They took your money?"

Florrie nodded. Her head hurt from bouncing off the brick wall, and things were still spinning a little. She felt sick, but she wasn't going to throw up in front of her brother. His eyes narrowed.

"They hurt you more than your face, didn't they?"

"Preston…"

He growled something and let go of her abruptly, making her sway. Then he began to pace around the room.

"I can't believe it. They came here and attacked you. I told them to leave you alone, that you had nothing to do with it."

Florrie was confused as to what was going on.

"What are you saying?"

"I had a bit of an argument with some young thugs who thought they were better than me. We got into a fight a few nights ago, and I won. One of them threatened to hurt both of us because of what I did."

Florrie groaned.

"You were out fighting? Preston, I thought you said you weren't going to do anything stupid…"

"I didn't go out looking for a fight, Florrie! I was minding my own business, and one of them decided to show off to his friends. They just picked the wrong person to try it on, that's all." Preston scowled. "I said that I wouldn't commit any further trouble, so could you listen to me on that?"

"I'd love to if I hadn't heard what you did," she shot back. Her head was throbbing, so she sagged onto a chair. "Now they've taken my wages, which I was going to use for the rent later in the week. It's gone up again and all of it was going to the landlord."

"And I won't get my money until the day after."

"Which is why I'm scared about what's going to happen. That man will throw us out if we don't have the money for him when he arrives: he's threatened to do it before, you know."

"He can't do that, can he?"

Florrie nodded. She knew the landlord would absolutely do it. Unlike his father, he was a horrible human being. He didn't care if he got his money, and he would be happy to humiliate anyone who got in the way. He tried with Florrie, and now she could tell he was looking for a way to do that with her since she turned down the offer of paying off her rent another way.

She would never lower herself to that.

"So what happens now?" Preston asked. He looked frustrated, fury blazing in his eyes. "I can't ask for my wages to be paid a day or two early, otherwise there would be a riot."

"He knows that which is why he has the rent money coming out the day before. He wants us to squirm."

"He would throw children into the streets?"

Florrie snorted.

"I'm not a child anymore, and you're not far off. We'd be homeless, for certain. Mrs. Irons won't have any extra room for us, and every other house on the street is filled. I can't see anyone bringing us in to help us out."

"There has to be a way." Preston hesitated. "There is a way, in fact. If you'll just let me…"

"No."

"You don't know what I'm going to say."

"I know exactly where your mind is going." Florrie shook her head, grimacing as it made things spin a little more. "You're not going to steal from anyone, especially not around here. If anyone finds out what you've done, you'll get beaten up yourself."

Preston huffed.

"It would be for survival, to get us out of this hole we've been thrown into. People will understand if we tell them."

"You think that's going to happen? I highly doubt it, and I don't want to be put in a position where we're known as thieves."

"Even so..." Preston went on, but Florrie cut him off.

"Do you think that it will keep us hidden from Credge? We've been lucky so far with everyone around us saying they don't know who we are, but the moment we betray their trust, we open ourselves up to being found, and then we have that supposed debt to deal with. We'll be right back where we started."

"Well, can you think of anything better?" Preston shot back. "You can't exactly go back to Mrs. Irons and ask her to pay you again. That's out of the question."

"I won't have you labelling us as thieves, Preston!" Florrie cried.

They glared at each other, both simmering with rage. Florrie wanted to give in and let her brother do what he said he could do, but it was too dangerous. With people who were decent to them living nearby and being patient with the fact the two of them were trying to make a go of it on their own, if things changed and they saw them as troublemakers, they would lose that sense of community.

Florrie hadn't been able to appreciate it until recently. Now she didn't want to lose it.

A knock at the door made them both jump, and Preston snatched up a knife from the table, holding it tightly as he went towards the door, padding softly so his footsteps wouldn't be heard. Florrie felt as if she was going to panic again. Was that the group of thugs who had attacked her? Had they come back to finish the job?

Or, God forbid, was it the landlord coming to demand rent earlier than normal? At this point, it wouldn't surprise her.

"Florrie? Are you in there?"

The voice took her by surprise. Nolan? What was he doing here? In the few months since meeting again, Florrie had made sure he didn't know where she lived. She had been adamant about keeping it from him, shame driving her to do so. It didn't matter if they had feelings for each other, she didn't want to be embarrassed by what little she had.

Nolan might've said otherwise, but she didn't want to get to that point.

Preston glanced at her in confusion. She shook her head. What was she supposed to say? She was just as stunned as him.

"Florrie?" Nolan was beginning to sound concerned. "Florrie, please answer me. Someone said you'd been hurt. If you're unconscious..."

"I'm fine, Nolan." The words were out of Florrie's mouth before she could stop them. "You don't need to worry about me."

"How about you let me be the judge of that? Can you open the door?"

Preston's eyes narrowed at her, his expression saying everything. He didn't want someone crossing the threshold. Florrie didn't want it, either. Getting up and wobbling a little, she grabbed her coat and limped over to the door.

"I'm coming out," she said. "One moment."

"Why is he here?" Preston hissed. "Did you tell me where we lived?"

"Of course not," Florrie whispered back. "I won't let him inside. At least trust me on that."

Preston didn't look happy, but he nodded and stepped away, lowering the knife but still scowling. Relieved that he wasn't questioning her further - that would be for later - Florrie opened the door and slipped outside, trying not to reveal too much to Nolan as he waited outside. His eyes widened when he saw her.

"My goodness!" he breathed.

"It's not that bad," Florrie said, attempting to deflect. "You don't need to worry."

"No need to worry?" Nolan's eyes scoured her face, his shock evident. "I can't believe anyone would do this to a woman. They're such cowards. Did they take anything from you?"

Florrie hesitated. She shouldn't be telling him anything about it beyond the basic details. And she certainly couldn't tell him what had been stolen. But if she did hide it, the truth would come out eventually, and Nolan would find out how dire her situation was. He knew things were not great, but if he discovered…

She felt ashamed. How could she have thought it would be all right to be acquainted with someone who was of a different social class to her? Nolan might've expressed interest in her and they were, essentially, courting, but when it came to making it more serious, they wouldn't be able to go any further with it. It was not going to work.

She should be walking away from him, but Florrie found that she couldn't.

"Oh, Florrie." Nolan's expression softened as he reached for her. "Come here."

She didn't have much chance to protest before he drew her into his arms, holding her gently as he slowly rocked her. Before she knew it, the tears were falling, and Florrie sobbed into his chest. She couldn't stop herself; it just came out and wouldn't stop.

Now she couldn't feel more humiliated. Preston could probably hear her sobbing through the door, which made Florrie want to curl into a ball and hide away from everyone. She was always the one who had to be strong, who had to figure things out on her own. But now this was happening, and she had no idea what she was supposed to do. She felt battered, tired, and fed up.

So fed up with everything.

"Don't cry, Florrie." Nolan kissed her head. "It's going to be all right."

"How do you know?" she croaked. "You don't know if things are going to be any better for me."

"I know it will be. I have faith in it." He eased her head up, resting his forehead against hers. "I'll make sure of it. You and I are going to be in this together. Whatever you need, I'm right there for you. I promise."

Florrie wanted to ask him about leaving for India, but it felt like the wrong time. Right now, she wanted to believe that Nolan was right, and things were going to be fine for her. She needed that right now.

A bit of belief just to help her carry on. Otherwise, the despair was going to be too much for her.

CHAPTER 8

"Where are you off to?" Preston asked.

Florrie turned away from the small mirror to see Preston looking at her from the chair by the fire. He had his jacket across his lap, and he was sewing a patch onto the elbow. She was glad she had told him that he needed to do his own darning because she had too much to do.

"I'm going out with Nolan again," she replied.

Preston looked bemused.

"You've been seeing him quite a lot lately, haven't you?"

"Why shouldn't I?"

"I feel like you're spending all your time with him. I hardly see you anymore."

Florrie rolled her eyes.

"You weren't worried about that before, Preston. Why should you be concerned now?"

"I just want to be sure you're not attacked again, Florrie. Your bruises have only just started to disappear."

Florrie did her best not to bring her hand up to touch her face. The bruises had faded after a while, but they had been gruesome. Mrs. Irons had been worried that clients would be concerned upon seeing her face and not wanting to bring their mending to her, thinking that they would bring trouble. Florrie had done her best to keep out of the way, keeping her head down and working.

When she got paid her wages, she practically ran home as quickly as she could, not wanting to be out in the open for long. The only time she did that was when she walked out with Nolan. He looked after her.

At least she hadn't been mugged again, but the issue of rent was still there. Despite appeasing the landlord briefly, he had a close eye on them now. Florrie knew they couldn't miss another payment, or they'd be out on the streets. She wasn't going to let them go to the workhouse.

"I'll be fine. Nolan won't let anything happen to me."

"I hope not," Preston grunted. "I don't want to have to deal with him because he hurt you. You deserve some happiness in your life, Florrie."

Her heart softened at that. It wasn't often she got nice compliments from her brother. Normally, he would just grunt at her.

"Well, you don't have to be so worried about me. I know what I'm doing."

She left before he could give her a response and headed outside. Nolan was already there, holding a small bouquet of flowers. Florrie gasped in delight when she saw them.

"Oh, Nolan, they're lovely."

"Beautiful flowers for a beautiful woman." He smiled as he held them out. "Something for us on our walk."

"I should put them in water, though."

But Florrie didn't want to waste time going back into the house to put them into a makeshift vase. That would just have Preston questioning her again. She wanted to spend as much time as possible with Nolan. He was still heading out on one of his father's ships, and he was delaying it as much as possible.

There was only so much he could do before he was forced onto a ship and set sail.

She didn't want that to happen. That would break her heart. Would she ever see him again? Florrie didn't know. She just knew, for certain, that she couldn't love anyone like she loved Nolan. If he was gone...

No, she wasn't going to think about that. It would just upset her, and she didn't want to be crying when in his company.

"Come on." Nolan held out an arm, which she took. "Let's go for a walk. There's a fudge stand further up the canal that I came across on my way home last time. I want to show it to you."

"I haven't had fudge in a long time."

"You'll love it. It's mouthwatering." Nolan chuckled. "Provided you don't put a whole cube into your mouth. Then your shirt ends up getting covered in drool because it's too big."

Florrie giggled.

"That sounds like you're speaking from personal experience."

"Let's just say that it's very easy to forget something like that when you want a delicious sweet in your mouth." Nolan leaned over and kissed her cheek. "I know you'll love it."

Florrie felt her face getting warm. They were out in public, and several of her neighbours were out and about. They kept giving her strange looks whenever they saw her walking around with Nolan, and she knew they were wondering what was going on.

Nolan was normally the perfect gentleman, but when he kissed her cheek or hand, even embracing her as he dropped her home, she became aware of people looking at them. Florrie didn't like being under such scrutiny. She loved him, and Nolan had made it clear over several weeks that he felt the same way, so why weren't they allowed to show it. The fact they were clearly of different social classes shouldn't matter at all.

It was very annoying.

"I've got some news about my departure," Nolan said, his tone solemn as they reached the end of the street and turned towards the bridge. "I've got to leave by the end of the month."

"What?" Florrie stopped and stared at him. "Why then?"

"That's when the next ship goes out, and it's heading to India. Father wants me to be on it, and he'll make sure that I am." He made a face. "Even if I have to be dragged on by the rest of the crew and chained up in the cells to keep me there."

"He can't do that, can he?"

"I'm afraid he can."

Florrie felt a flash of annoyance. She hadn't met any of Nolan's family, but she was aware of how strict and cruel his father was. He wanted things done a certain way, and that had put plenty of people's backs up. Nolan didn't like it, ranting enough about it to Florrie when they were together. He preferred it when his uncle was in charge. Unfortunately, unless something happened to his father, there wasn't anything he could do about it.

Florrie had hoped, over time, Nolan's father would forget about sending his son away and realise that he needed him around. But that wasn't happening. The end of the month was only two weeks away.

"Can't you just say you are staying no matter what?" she protested. "You've managed to do it so far."

"There's another factor in this."

"What?"

Nolan hesitated. Florrie didn't like it when he drip-fed her news this way. She wanted to be told immediately. She stopped walking and glared at him with her arms folded.

"You tell me exactly what's going on, Nolan Baxter. I'm not moving another inch until you tell me."

"He found out about us."

Florrie faltered.

"What? He knows about you and me courting?"

Nolan nodded, glancing away and running his fingers

through his hair. He looked very unhappy, and Florrie saw the pain in his face.

"I didn't tell him anything, and I wasn't planning to just yet, but one of his employees saw us in the market the other day, and they told him about it. Especially with how close I was to you. It was clear to anyone that I was there in a romantic sense with you."

Florrie winced. She could imagine the fallout from that.

"He didn't take it well, did he?"

"Of course he didn't," Nolan snorted. "He was furious about it. Said that he had someone picked out for me once I returned from India, and that I would marry that girl. I had no business getting involved with a seamstress." He held up his hands. "I'm only saying what he told me, Florrie."

"That's why he wants you to be on the ship soon," Florrie murmured. "I'm surprised he didn't make you get on the first available one."

"I think he would've tried, but that was the first one out that had the room for me. I've told him no, but I'm going regardless of what I want." Nolan took a deep breath, his jaw tight. "I can't believe I still have to have my life dictated to me. I thought he would leave me be and let me make my own choices, but he's been arranging something for me behind my back. I can't do it anymore, but…"

Florrie knew what he was going to say. He didn't like it, and wanted to fight back, but there was only so much he could do. Nolan's father could take everything away from him with a snap of his fingers, and Nolan wouldn't be able to do anything about it. Her heart ached for him. She thought she had few options for her life going forward, but at least her father hadn't been cruel towards her. In fact, he had been loving. From what Nolan told her; he hadn't been able to have any of that. His uncle showed him kindness, so he saw him more as a father figure.

"What did he threaten you with?" she asked. "Why did he say to get you onto the ship?"

"That he would disinherit me."

"What? He'd leave you with nothing because of me?"

Nolan nodded grimly.

"He said that he would have me cut out of the will entirely, and that it would happen if I didn't go to India, or if I continued to see you. I've had to slip away to see you today, to tell you what's going on."

"And…" Florrie hesitated, her chest tightening. "Does this mean you're going to stop seeing me now?"

"No, of course not!" He reached for her, and clasped her hands, his fingers warm through his gloves. "I love you, Florrie. I don't want to be apart from you for any reason, but I am scared that Father will turn his wrath on you if he figures that you're still in my life. I know he can make things difficult for you."

Florrie scoffed at that.

"I've got Father's creditor still chasing me despite everything. I don't think you have to worry on that account. I can cope."

"You haven't met him. Father is…very good at getting what he wants. And he wants me to go to India." He swallowed, pulling her closer. "I can't bear to be away from you, but I can't take you with me. I wish I could, but that won't be possible."

"If only we could do something about it." Florrie leaned her forehead against his. "I wish there was something."

"Well, there's only so much we can do, but I intend to follow through on everything." He kissed her. "First, Florrie, I want you to have my savings."

"What?" She pulled back from him. "What did you say?"

"I won't be able to take my savings with me, and it would be just like Father to take it away from me while I'm away. I know he's capable of doing it." Nolan shook his head. "Even after everything, he still controls me. But if I give you my savings…"

"I can't accept that!"

"You won't have to worry about your rent. There's more than enough to pay your rent for the time I'm away, and then to get a little bit more that you need to live on. Then you and Preston can have your wages for something better. Maybe you can buy some new clothes or buy something to brighten up your home. If I know you're not going to be thrown out onto the streets..."

"But what about when you come back?" Florrie pointed out. "What are you going to do then?"

"I'll have my own money. I'll be getting paid for this work. Then when I return, I'll have more than enough for us to leave and get married." He raised her hands to his mouth and kissed her fingers, his eyes never leaving her face. "We talked about getting married, didn't we?"

"Yes..."

"Once I return, I'll whisk you away and we'll marry. You and I can be together properly. Preston can come with us until he can stand on his own two feet, but you and I...we won't have to worry about anything else."

Florrie remembered when Nolan said he wanted to marry her, but she hadn't given much thought to it. Now clarity was setting in. He did want to be with her, truly. Despite the despair knowing they were going to be separated, she felt happy in the knowledge she would be Nolan's wife.

She kissed him.

"We can talk about marriage, and what we're going to do," she said. "But I don't want you to forget me, Nolan."

He smiled at him.

"I love you, Florrie. I'm not going to be forgetting you at all."

She believed him, especially when she looked into his eyes. He really meant it.

CHAPTER 9

Florrie stood at the window and looked out into the street. It was looking busier today with more barges coming along the river. She wondered if something big was going on or was business picking up more than usual. It would be good for Preston, now he was working further upstream. It would be good for him to get more work.

"Is something the matter, Florrie?" Mrs. Irons asked, looking up from her sewing. "You've been standing there in a daydream for a while now."

"Sorry, Mrs. Irons." Florrie turned away from the window. "I was just thinking about my brother. He's going to be grumpy when he gets home, complaining about his legs."

The seamstress laughed.

"Well, he got a job as a legger, it's his fault. But at least he'll get decent pay with the extra boats going back and forth, and it's a stable job."

Florrie had thought Preston was talking nonsense when he told her about it. He had said he was to be a legger, and it didn't sound right. Apparently, the tunnels along the canals weren't big enough for the horses pulling the boats along to get through, so they employed people to wait at the tunnels and use their legs against the wall to move the boats down the narrow gap. Florrie wondered why they wouldn't just make the tunnels wider, but that would've cost more money from what Preston said. He said it was something different and because they needed them all the time it would keep him out of trouble.

She was glad that he was taking the initiative not to do anything stupid. He still wanted to go and steal things, but he was determined to not let his sister down. Florrie could see him becoming a more manageable, mature young man. She hoped he stayed the course.

"At least it keeps him out of trouble," Mrs. Irons continued, giving Florrie a slight smile. "He can't run away if his legs hurt too much."

"Mrs. Irons!"

"He's just like any other youngster in the area. Always trying to do something different to bring the money in. We all feel sorry for them, but there's only so much we can do when we don't get much ourselves." The older woman shrugged. "You'll understand when you're a bit older, Florrie dear. Things are not as secret as you think about here."

Florrie didn't know what to say about that. She wondered if that meant they all knew about Credge being a creditor looking to get money off her. As far as she was aware, Credge herself hadn't found her and Preston, although she was sure the mugging from last month was something to do with her. She wouldn't be surprised, at this point.

But if Mrs. Irons knew about it, and she hadn't said a thing, did that mean she was being supportive and helping her? Florrie hoped that was the case; she didn't want to have someone turning on her.

Picking up her sewing, she started again. However, Florrie couldn't get her mind to stop wandering, and she found herself thinking about Nolan. She hadn't seen him for two days, not since he had been caught sneaking out of the house to see her. He'd managed to send her a note by the boot boy, but he couldn't leave himself. His father was keeping him under lock and key, not wanting him to be seen with Florrie again.

That had worried her sick, and she wanted to go to his house to plead his case, but Nolan had urged her not to. He would write to her and see her again once he returned. She didn't even know which ship he was sailing out of, or what port. Florrie felt miserable knowing that he was leaving in a couple of days and she wouldn't see him for a year.

Why couldn't they have gotten married before he left? It would've made sense, but Nolan had said waiting for the special license would take too long, and he didn't want it to be rushed. Florrie had to agree with that, although she wished she had insisted. Or even driven up to Gretna Green.

By carriage, it would be a couple of days, and nobody could stop them then. But she had to think about what was going on around her, and Nolan pointed out while Mrs. Irons might be amenable she might not keep Florrie on if she disappeared for a couple of days.

She hated that she was stuck in this position.

A loud banging at the door made her jump, and the needle stabbed her in the finger. Mrs. Irons looked up in surprise.

"What on earth?" Putting her work aside, she hurried over to the window and looked out. "What's happening out there?"

"Perhaps something's gone wrong on the canal?" Florrie asked, sucking her sore finger. "Maybe something happened to your husband?"

"I can't tell, the door is out of sight. I'll let them in."

Mrs. Irons left, and Florrie heard the front door opening and hurried voices, not quite loud enough for her to hear what was being said. Then someone came rushing in.

"Florrie!"

It took her a moment to realise that it was Nolan. Before

Florrie could react to what she was seeing, he had fallen to his knees and pulled her into a tight embrace. Florrie gasped in pain and pushed against him.

"The needle! Ouch!"

"Oh!" Nolan pulled back quickly. "Sorry! I didn't…"

Florrie flinched as she pulled the needle from the flesh of her finger. She had done it plenty of times over the years, but it still hurt. Flexing her hand, she put her sewing to one side and looked at Mrs. Irons, who had stuck her head into the room.

"I'll just give you a moment, Mr. Baxter," she said, giving him a nod. "Don't be too long, though."

"I promise I won't be, Mrs. Irons."

The seamstress left, and Florrie grabbed Nolan's head to make him look at her. His eyes were bright, and his cheeks flushed, his breath coming out in pants. He must've run all the way from his house.

"What is going on, Nolan? You're supposed to be locked up at home. I thought I wasn't going to…"

"I'm not going."

Florrie blinked.

"What? Why not? Did your father finally agree to let you stay here?"

"No, nothing like that." He swallowed and looked slightly chastened. "I feel guilty for being like this, especially given the circumstances, but…"

"But what? You're not making any sense, Nolan."

"Father's dead."

It took a moment for the words to sink in. Florrie wondered if she had misheard him, but as she stared at him, his expression didn't change. Nothing shifted to say that she had heard him wrong.

"I beg your pardon?" she croaked. "Your father is dead. But how?"

"We were having dinner last night, and he was eating and

drinking as normal. Then he started shouting at me, telling me I was going to ruin his life..."

Nolan broke off, and she saw the distress seeping in. He looked close to tears. Florrie realised, despite what had happened between father and son, he still loved the man. It was hard to turn off that type of love when they were family.

It caused Florrie think about her own father, someone who had been loving towards his wife and children and then left them in immense debt. She loved him, but she didn't like him for what he'd done. Nolan had admitted he felt the same way about his father.

Now he was gone, and he was clearly going to feel conflicted. Florrie tugged him onto the chair beside her.

"Take it slowly," she said gently. "You don't need to rush through it."

"I know. It's just..." He took a few deep breaths, trying to calm himself. "It's not something I'm used to, someone dying in front of me. He was angry at me one minute, calling me a failure and he wasn't going to have me around, and then he was clutching at his chest, trying to breathe and get his words out."

"But how?"

"The doctor came immediately, but it was still too late." He spoke as if he hadn't heard her. "He said that Father suffered a heart attack. It was very quick, and by the time he realised what was going on, it would've been too late."

"Oh, my." Florrie's hand went to her mouth. "That's awful. I know those come on suddenly. Was your father in poor health before?"

"Not really. He liked to think that he was relatively healthy, but the doctor said he needed to stop eating and drinking to excess, that it could make things difficult for him in the future. Father simply ignored him, saying he was going to enjoy life regardless."

"And it caught up with him." Florrie laid her hand on his.

"Nolan, I'm so sorry. I know you two didn't get along, but he was your father. How's your mother taking it?"

"She's in shock. She didn't think he was going to die like that, especially in front of us. We didn't know what to do." Nolan sat up and took a deep breath. "It means that, because Father didn't update his will to cut me out, I inherit the family business. I'm in charge now."

He still sounded in a daze about it. Florrie grasped onto that, trying to get him back to reality.

"That means you don't need to go to India now, doesn't it? You can stay here?"

"Absolutely. I'm not going anywhere." He looked at her, and Florrie saw the intensity in his expression. "I have a business to run and sort out, and I also have someone in my life that I intend to keep. It's a lot easier when I don't live too far away as well."

"Nolan..."

"I know this isn't an ideal time for it, and I'll understand if you want to wait a bit longer, but you're the woman I want in my life, Florrie." He turned to face her, grasping both of her hands. "I want you to be my wife, the woman at my side. I love you, and that's not going to change. You're it for me, and I want to show to everyone that's what I want."

Florrie could feel her hesitation. After all, the circumstances were not ideal at all, and she felt uncomfortable about it. But she couldn't pass this on, grasping the knowledge that Nolan was staying in England, and that he would be here with her.

She felt her heart lighten knowing that she wouldn't have to worry about him in another country, right across the world.

"I love you, Nolan. I think you know the answer."

"I still want to hear it. Please."

That made her smile, and Florrie hugged him tightly.

"Yes. And it's always going to be yes."

CHAPTER 10

"I feel very nervous about this," Florrie said, adjusting her dress again. Nolan took her hand and pulled it away from her collar.

"Stop fiddling around with that, otherwise it's going to break, and you'll be left in just your petticoat."

"I can't help it. I'm meeting your mother, after all."

"She's not scary. You don't have to be worried about her."

"Even so, it's only been a few days since your father was buried," Florrie protested. "She might think it was inappropriate to come by with your future wife. It'll be embarrassing to go through that scrutiny."

Nolan sighed and put an arm around her shoulders.

"I know you're nervous, and I am, too. But I can't keep hiding you away like some sort of dirty secret. It's only fair that she knows about you. Besides, she's been asking about you, and I know she wants to meet you."

"Really?"

"Absolutely. She's keen to see the person who's been making me smile and be happier than normal. Father might've been against the courtship, but she isn't."

Florrie didn't know what to say about that. She wasn't sure what to think at this moment. When Nolan had come to her, just two days after burying his father, saying that his mother wanted to meet her, she was immediately confused and concerned. Was this his way of getting her into his life by meeting his mother? And wasn't it a little inappropriate to do it so soon after a death? Florrie didn't know anymore.

But she did want to get on with Mrs. Baxter. Nolan had spoken about her in glowing terms, but he would say anything to make her feel better about meeting the woman of the man she loved.

However, when she expressed these thoughts to Preston, hoping that she wasn't going about this the wrong way, he simply told her to stop thinking too much. She was worrying over something Nolan had dealt with, and she should trust him. It was a little startling to have her brother on Nolan's side, but Florrie had decided to trust her fiancé.

Even if she couldn't stop the thoughts from going around inside her head and making her feel like her stomach was in knots.

"Just breathe," Nolan said gently, taking her hand and squeezing it as they walked. "Mother will love you, I promise. Just like I love you."

"Does she know that you've proposed to me?"

"Not yet, but I'll talk to her about it. I'm sure she's figured this out already, given how I've been. She says that she doesn't want to see me miserable again."

That made Florrie feel a little better. She hoped that Mrs. Baxter would continue to feel like that as things went on. She didn't want to make a mess of it.

Nolan's home was further away from the canal, a standalone home with a wide driveway and vast gardens. He had described his house, but Florrie hadn't anticipated anything like this. She could help but feel the gulf between them in terms of social class as they walked up the driveway.

But she didn't dwell on it for long. She wasn't about to do something that would put a dampener on her love for Nolan. She knew this was real, and she wanted to keep hold of it, but seeing where he grew up was a little startling.

It would be better, she hoped. She could get used to living somewhere like this. It would be the first time living in such a big house, one that wasn't just one or two rooms. It was something that would be a shock to her, but Florrie knew she could manage it. Eventually.

She just needed to get Mrs. Baxter's approval first.

Once Nolan let them in, he led her into the drawing room. A handsome woman with fair hair and a buxom appearance, wearing a simple but elegant black dress, was sitting at a writing desk by the window. She looked up as Nolan and Florrie entered and smiled when she saw Nolan.

"There you are! I was beginning to think you were never coming home."

"What did you think I was doing, Mother?"

"I don't know, but I was starting to wonder." Putting her pen down, the woman stood and walked towards them, her gaze now on Florrie. "So, this is your lovely seamstress, is it?"

"This is Florrie." Nolan sounded proud as he put an arm around her waist. "Florrie, this is my mother, Margaret Baxter."

Dropping her eyes to the floor, Florrie curtsied.

"Nice to meet you, Mrs. Baxter."

"It's Margaret, dear. You don't need to be so formal. And it's lovely to meet you after all this time." Margaret wagged a finger at Nolan. "This boy knows how to make things awkward. He kept you a secret for a long time, although for good reason. I'm just glad he's coming around to introducing you."

Florrie looked at Nolan, whose cheeks had gone a little red. Clearing his throat, he led Florrie over to the settee.

"I'm sorry about coming over so soon after your husband's funeral," Florrie said hurriedly. "And I'm very sorry for your loss."

"Thank you, dear. We all had a feeling he was going to end up getting into serious trouble with his health with the way he was going, but he was too stubborn and refused to do anything about it. Said that he would be fine." Margaret sighed. "I'm afraid it caught up with him. We knew it would happen, but to see it…"

"I don't want to cause you further distress, Mrs. Baxter," Florrie added, embarrassed that they were going down a difficult conversation. "I apologise for any further discomfort."

But the other woman smiled.

"You don't need to worry about anything, my dear. We all deal with grief in different ways. And I'd like to do it getting to know the woman who's caught my son's attention. That takes a special person to do that with Nolan."

"Mother," Nolan mumbled. "You're going to make me blush."

Margaret laughed.

"It would serve you right, keeping this lovely young thing to yourself. Why don't you ask Mrs. Finchley when she's going to bring the tea in? I'd like to talk to Florrie alone."

Nolan looked nervous about leaving Florrie, but she gave him a reassuring smile.

"Don't worry. I'll be fine."

He seemed to listen, and he squeezed her hand before leaving the room. Florrie couldn't help but giggle.

"He was telling me not to be worried when I come to visit, and here he is nervous about leaving me alone."

"Nolan's been going back and forth between the two emotions since I suggested that you came to visit. He's worried that things are going to go wrong, but he's adamant about not letting you go." Margaret paused. "I think he's more frightened that you would leave him. You have more power over him than you realise."

"Really?"

"I know it would break his heart if he lost you. He was certainly close to it when my husband said that he was to set sail for India as soon as he could."

"I wouldn't want to leave him," Florrie said quickly, trying to reassure her. "I love Nolan. I didn't anticipate it happening between us, but it did. And to know he's not leaving, that he's going to stay here...it feels like someone was listening to my prayers."

"I understand that feeling all too well. You never want the man you loved to walk away, otherwise it might just break you." Margaret sighed. "I used to feel like that, many years ago. And then I had to get married, and my heart broke anyway."

That caught Florrie by surprise. Hadn't her husband been the love of her life?

"But...your husband..."

"It was an arranged marriage, much like the one he tried to set up for Nolan. He wanted to make sure it was as advantageous as possible, but Nolan kept fighting it. Even before you came into his life, he knew what he wanted." Margaret shook her head. "My husband was a stubborn man. I'll miss him and he did have his good points, but I did wish he would open his eyes and see that life doesn't go as you want. I could see how hard it was for Nolan, and I tried to be on his side, but that's harder than you think."

Florrie thought about Credge, and how persistent she had been over the years. She had the decision made up in her head, and she wasn't about to be persuaded otherwise. Something about Mr. Baxter reminded her of the nasty woman. It was easier said than done to get away from a person like that.

"Nolan says he's not going to India anymore," she said. "That he's going to stay here."

"He is, thank God. I don't like the idea of him going halfway across the world." Margaret shook her head. "I'm afraid he has his work cut out with the business, though. It's not going to be as simple as just taking over."

"What do you mean?"

"His uncle, my brother-in-law, was a good businessman. He was harsh but fair, and he knew how to keep everyone in line. Unfortunately, my husband didn't have the same ability. He knew how to run a business, but with the iron fist that his father had before. It's made the employees rebel, and they've started doing corrupt dealings under the table just so they can get by."

Florrie stared.

"They started stealing from the business?"

"You could say that. I don't know how much of it my husband knew, but if I was aware of it then he had to be. It's going to be quite a mess to clear up, and I don't know if Nolan can cope with tidying things up."

"Of course I can cope." Nolan's voice behind them made both women jump. He shook his head with a wry smile as he crossed the room. "You need to have more faith in me, Mother. It's not as dreadful as you think."

"Do you mean about the business?" she asked.

"About me knowing how to manage things. I've been aware of the corruption for quite some time, and I know these men can be reasonable." He sat beside Florrie and took her hand. "It's going to be rough, but I can manage. Anyway, shall we talk about something more interesting and less depressing?"

"Of course." Margaret cleared her throat and dusted down her skirts. "Forgive me, I'm still meant to be in mourning. Depressing thoughts seem to be par of the course."

"Well, we've got some good news for you." Nolan squeezed Florrie's hand. "I'm sure you can be happy with that."

Florrie frowned at him. Had he said something about them getting married? Nolan had said he'd told his mother about her, but had he mentioned the engagement? It would be a big shock if they told her now.

"Oh, you mean about your engagement?" Margaret smiled. "I'm sure that will keep my mind fully occupied."

"You're not upset about it?" Florrie questioned nervously.

"Why should I be? My son has found someone he loves, and it's only the next natural step. Naturally, the timing of it all when he's meant to be in mourning is a little off, but we can work around that. You don't have to worry about anything when it comes to that."

Florrie managed a smile, but her stomach was churning to the point she felt very uncomfortable. She hoped that they would talk about something else because she was sure she was going to get something wrong.

She wanted to marry Nolan. There was no doubt in her mind about it, but, as Margaret said, the timing was not good. What were people going to say about it once the engagement was announced? And would Nolan change his mind once he heard everyone's reaction to it?

"You can stop going turning it over in your mind, darling," Nolan said gently, giving her a knowing look.

"Pardon?"

"I can see the cogs turning. You're worried that I might walk away from you if the reception isn't as good as I want it."

Florrie felt her face getting warm. How did he know that's what she was concerned about? He chuckled and brought her hand to his mouth, kissing her fingers. His look was loving; affection clear in his eyes.

"You don't have to worry about that. I'm not going anywhere, and I hope you don't think that this will end abruptly because of something that's not anyone else's business?"

"I'm not, but..."

"It's natural for her to be nervous, Nolan," Margaret said before Florrie could get any further. "But as long as you remain true to what you want, and don't disrespect Florrie, then she should be calmer. Especially if she sees you follow through."

"I plan to."

He sounded certain about that, and Florrie knew she could trust him. Her fears were being validated, but at least she wasn't being dismissed as being silly. Nolan and Margaret were good people, and they were treating her kindly.

She could see herself getting used to being a part of their family very easily.

CHAPTER 11

"Preston!" Margaret called. "Where are you?"

There was a rustling of leaves, and then Preston's voice came from above their heads.

"I'm up here, Mrs. Baxter!"

Margaret frowned.

"What are you doing in the tree?"

"I'm just getting the last of the apples. They're right at the top."

"You need to be careful! You're not as young as you used to be. You could fall."

Preston simply started laughing. Sitting beside Margaret, Florrie smiled.

"You don't need to worry about him, Margaret. Preston's probably the most agile person I've ever met. Nothing's going to happen to him."

"That's famous last words, dear." Her future mother-in-law didn't look so happy as she sat back in her chair. "He's practically a grown man now, and those apple trees aren't as sturdy as you think."

"At least it's keeping him busy."

The older woman seemed to agree with that. When they had met the first time, four months before, they had discussed how things were going to work. Florrie had asked what would happen to Preston, worried that he would relapse into crime if she wasn't around, and Margaret had offered to let him come along as well. Preston had been dubious about being accepted so readily, and had been adamant about earning his keep, claiming it would keep him busy. So, Margaret had offered to let him help out with the garden.

To everyone's surprise, most of all Florrie's, Preston thrived in working in the garden. He tended to the flowers and trimmed the hedges without complaint, and he was happy toiling away outside. The head gardener was impressed by him, and within a few weeks Preston was getting paid and became a junior gardener.

Florrie had wondered what people would think about that, having her brother work for her husband's family, but Margaret and Nolan urged her to leave it be. If Preston was happy, and he clearly was, then there was no need to change it.

She was still nervous about what people would say, but she loved seeing her brother looking content for the first time in his life.

"His birthday is coming up soon, isn't it?" Margaret asked suddenly, pouring out another cup of tea for herself.

Florrie stared.

"Yes, in two weeks."

"I'm very good at remembering birthdays. And I like to get the person in question a nice gift. You're his sister, so you know him better than me."

Florrie bit her lip, suddenly feeling embarrassed.

"I don't know if I can answer that. I feel a little ashamed that I don't know what he likes."

"Did you not give each other gifts on your birthday?"

"Very rarely. We...we couldn't afford it."

Margaret tittered.

"Whoever failed you in the past did you a great disservice. You really should have time to celebrate birthdays, Christmas and Easter."

"That was easier said than done."

Florrie had told Margaret about Credge and how she was still chasing them for a debt she was sure had been paid off. Margaret had been horrified knowing that someone was harassing children when she should have written the debt off. She declared it was just cruel. Nothing more had been said beyond that, which made Florrie wonder if the older woman was plotting something. She was very good at that; there was something about her that reminded her of Nolan.

She wondered how he was getting on. Nolan had gone to the docks to the main offices so he could have a closer look at the accounts. The business' accountant would be waiting for him, and they would be figuring out where the money was going.

While things were going well enough, Nolan couldn't afford to have thieves in his employ. He was nervous about dismissing anyone, but they all knew it had to be done. Florrie hoped they would sort something out and make things better for all of them. It wasn't fair to pay for what Mr. Baxter hadn't done.

"Margaret!"

Margaret looked over her shoulder, and Florrie saw a look of dismay pass across her face. A tall, slim woman wearing dark green with a matching hat and coat was walking across the terrace towards them. A small dog trotted at her side, looking like the world's strangest guard dog. The woman beamed at Margaret.

"There you are, darling! Your butler said you were outside, so I thought I'd come around the side instead of through the house."

"Mrs. Mayfield. It's nice to see you." Margaret absently brushed crumbs off her skirt. "I thought you were in the Lake District with your husband."

"Oh, we've just returned. It was gorgeous there. Not a drop of rain for days." Mrs. Mayfield tilted her golden head to one side. "We heard about your husband's death, though. We offer our condolences that we didn't hear about it sooner. If we'd heard sooner, we could've returned…"

"You mustn't put yourselves out for me," Margaret said hurriedly. "And thank you for your condolences."

Florrie watched the interaction between the two of them and wondered about their relationship. From Mrs. Mayfield's side, she seemed comfortable enough to walk into someone else's house without having to worry about anyone stopping her. With Margaret, she looked as if she would be rather somewhere else.

"Why don't you sit and have some tea with us?" Margaret said, a little too brightly.

"I think that's a splendid idea." Mrs. Mayfield sat on one of the remaining chairs and looked at Florrie. "And who's this young thing? I didn't know you had guests."

"This is Florence Walsh," Margaret replied, fiddling about with the cups. "She's Nolan's future bride."

The other woman's eyebrows shot up in evident surprise. Florrie felt as if she was under scrutiny again.

"Really? I thought he was going to marry Matilda Madsen. Your husband was talking about it."

"You think Nolan is going to marry someone he doesn't love? That boy wouldn't go through with that."

"I see." Mrs. Mayfield peered curiously at Florrie. "And what family are you from? I don't know of the Walsh family. Are you a newcomer to Manchester?"

"No, I was born here." She had no idea how her voice wasn't trembling. "I've lived in Manchester all my life."

The woman looked surprised. Her dog was sitting at her feet and seemed to be looking at her with a piercing stare. Florrie had never been judged by a dog like this, and she resisted the urge to squirm.

"You have?" Mrs. Mayfield looked at Margaret. "So where did Nolan meet her? I know everyone in our social circle, and there is certainly no Walsh family."

"I met Nolan when he came to collect something of his uncle's," Florrie said quickly. "His uncle was a customer of my seamstress business, and…"

"Seamstress?" Mrs. Mayfield squeaked. "You're a seamstress?" She pressed a hand to her chest in horror. "Margaret, you're not telling me that you're condoning this? Nolan shouldn't marry someone so common."

Florrie felt her face getting warm, and anger stirred in her belly. Margaret gave Mrs. Mayfield a haughty look.

"I don't think there's anything common at all. Florrie is a kind, decent young girl, and she loves my son deeply. That love is returned, and Nolan is devoted to her. Why wouldn't I support it if it makes him happy?"

"But what about your social standing? Aren't you worried about that?"

"Not everyone is concerned about social standing, Mrs. Mayfield. If you're not happy, then what's the point of it?"

Mrs. Mayfield spluttered, her face turning bright pink. If she hadn't been so upset with her remarks, Florrie was sure she would end up laughing at the sight. She had endured plenty of snobbery from more of Margaret's acquaintances, and she was getting fed up with it.

"How can you lower your family to this level?" Mrs. Mayfield gasped. "It's just…you shouldn't be doing it!"

"Why not?"

"Because she's not one of us!"

Margaret sighed and put the cups back where they had been.

"I think we don't have enough time for you to have tea with us, Mrs. Mayfield. Maybe you should send a calling card ahead and make an appointment to come to my home."

"What?" The woman looked confused. "You're asking me to leave? But I've only just sat down!"

"You insulted my future daughter-in-law within moments of arriving, and I will not tolerate that, especially in my house." Margaret's voice had suddenly gone cold. "I'm not about to allow that to happen."

"But she's..."

"So what if she's a seamstress? Does that take away from the fact she's a kind, generous young woman who has a heart of gold? It's not that difficult to show her some basic decency, is it? And yet you immediately went to worrying about how people are going to see us." Margaret got to her feet. "That is for my family to worry about, and if we're not concerned, you don't have to think about it. Just treat all my family the same, and there won't be a problem. Now, if you would please leave?"

"Well, I never!" Mrs. Mayfield sniffed, jumping to her feet. "I never thought I'd see you speak to me like that, Margaret! You were always such a shy creature. Wouldn't say anything out of turn."

"That's what happens when you have a husband like mine." Margaret smiled thinly. "He's not here anymore, and I'm not going to allow anyone else to be bullied in this house. Now, I would like you to leave because asking for you to apologise would be too much, wouldn't it?"

Mrs. Mayfield looked as if she was going to explode. Then she took a deep breath and squared her shoulders.

"I'm sorry for the way I spoke, Margaret." She did sound genuinely remorseful, although still a little stunned. "I didn't mean to cause offence."

"You did, but the fact you're apologising is helping you." Margaret turned to Florrie. "It's up to you, dear. What do you think we should do?"

Florrie didn't want the decision to be put on her, but she could see the contrition in the visitor's face. She didn't want to have the rest of the social circle in Manchester against them. She had to win them over somehow. Managing a smile, she began to set out the cups again.

"I'm sure Mrs. Mayfield can restart this visit," she said. "She must be dying to know what's been happening in her absence. And if she's genuinely sorry, then I don't see anything wrong with letting her stay for a while."

Both women looked surprised by her reaction. Margaret recovered first and she nodded, patting Florrie on the shoulder.

"We'll follow your example, dear. But I'll be there if you need her to leave."

"Thank you, Margaret. I do appreciate that."

Looking chastened, Mrs. Mayfield sat down again. Florrie would've laughed at the look on her face, but she didn't. Although she was sure she could hear Preston chuckling high up in the nearby apple tree. Ignoring her brother, she picked up the teapot.

"So, tell me, Mrs Mayfield. What business is it that your husband is in? And how do you know the Baxters?"

CHAPTER 12

1885

Florrie sat on the edge of the bed, pressing a hand to her stomach. It hadn't stopped churning, although she was not feeling sick anymore. She had finished throwing up, and she could taste the bile in her mouth.

What was wrong with her? She couldn't have eaten anything bad lately, although the smell of some of her favourite foods did set her off, and it was hampering her ability to carry on as normal.

Had she had some food poisoning recently? That couldn't be right; she, Nolan and Margaret had been eating the same things, and they were fine. So why was it just her?

Maybe she should go to the doctor and explain the situation. Perhaps he would know what to do. Florrie decided to head to the doctor before going to see her brother. No need to worry her husband and mother-in-law just yet.

Husband? That made Florrie smile. It had been four months since she and Nolan had finally gotten married, back in November. That had been the happiest day of Florrie's life, standing opposite Nolan and repeating her vows. Not something she ever expected to do, and yet it was happening.

Her life of poverty was over. Now she was comfortable and could leave her old life behind. Preston had urged her to, saying this was her way of having a fresh start.

She wasn't the only one. Preston had loved his job as a gardener, but he still felt uncomfortable working for Margaret and Nolan, so he had applied for a gardening job at another house. Mrs. Mayfield, much to everyone's surprise, had agreed to take him on as a trial basis, and now he was a full employee at her home.

Nobody had expected that, given the initial greeting the woman had given Florrie, but she appeared to have softened towards the siblings. Florrie had found she was a nice woman, and it was just society that had drummed things into her head. She was particularly fond of Preston, and she had agreed to take him on.

He was thriving, according to Preston when Florrie last saw him. He couldn't have found a better job, and he was growing as a person. It was a delight to see.

There was the issue of Credge still looking for them, and Florrie kept looking over her shoulder, wondering if she was going to find the woman standing there. It was a surprise that she hadn't come looking after the wedding, given that there was much talk about Nolan marrying a lowly seamstress. But nothing was happening yet.

She couldn't relax for a while, but at least Florrie felt more comfortable with her situation. Although she was concerned that Credge would appear and demand the debt be paid. She couldn't drag her family into that anymore. Credge would start demanding more, even though she'd taken more than she deserved.

A knock at the door made her jump.

"Florrie? Are you in there?"

It was Nolan. Florrie's spirits lifted. He had left two days ago to head over to Liverpool regarding the business. She had barely seen him over the last few days. Practically jumping off the bed, she hurried over to the door and unlocked it. Nolan stood there, looking dishevelled and tired, but more handsome than she remembered.

Florrie felt her heart swell with love as he pulled her into his arms and kissed her. Then he embraced her tightly, burying his face in her neck.

"I've missed you so much," he groaned.

"I've missed you, too." Florrie pulled back, smiling at him as she cupped his face in her hands. "You look exhausted."

"This does take it out of me, and all this travelling back and forth." Nolan made a face. "I hate it. It's just easier to manage when I'm in my study at home, but I have to be face-to-face with these people."

"But it's all sorted now?"

"For now. I've given myself a few days to rest properly. I'm going to need it." He kissed her. "I want to spend time with my wife. I feel like I've neglected you lately, and I feel awful for it."

"You don't have to worry about anything. I'm perfectly fine."

"Says the person who looks more exhausted than I am. Are you looking after yourself, Florrie?"

"I'm fine. You don't need to be concerned."

Even as she said that her stomach churned again, and Florrie felt lightheaded. She swayed on her feet, and Nolan caught her. Leading her over to the bed, he urged her to lie down. The lightheaded sensation was still there, but at least the room wasn't spinning. Florrie groaned and put her hands over her face.

"I don't know what's wrong with me. I've been feeling like this for some time."

"How long?"

"A few weeks."

Nolan looked aghast.

"A few weeks? But why wouldn't you tell me about it? You should've said something about it before."

"I didn't want to worry you. I thought it would simply pass. Besides, you've been incredibly busy lately, and I didn't want to get in the way."

"Don't be ridiculous!" he cried. "If you're in distress, you should've told me! Or Mother! You know she worries about you. I swear she's adopted you as her daughter and loves you more than me."

Florrie couldn't help but smile at that. He wasn't far off his assessment; Margaret had started treating Florrie like her own child, and it felt like having her mother back. She did miss her own mother, but it was nice to have someone who looked after her.

"Does Mother know about this?" Nolan went on.

She shook her head. He sighed and rubbed a hand over his face.

"Florrie, you need to talk to us. You keep doing as you did before you were married. You carry on as if it's just you dealing with it. But you've got me now. I can look after you. You don't have to do this it on your own."

"I understand that," Florrie protested.

"So, start talking to us. If you're sick, you need to tell us. The sooner we get it sorted, the sooner you can get better." He leaned over and kissed her forehead. "What matters is your health. I'm not going anywhere until I know you're better."

Florrie felt like she wanted to cry. She loved Nolan so much and hearing him say this was a shock to her, even after all this time. She couldn't believe that she had someone like him as her husband. That he would willingly lower himself down to her and take her as his wife. She was aware that she was being silly, and there was nothing wrong, but her head was always filled with a lot of doubt.

She was scared that it would be suddenly taken away from her.

"What's going on in your mind, darling?" Nolan brushed her hair from her face. "What are you thinking?"

"Nothing much."

"I can tell that's not quite true."

Florrie frowned.

"You shouldn't accuse a woman of lying. It's not nice."

"You know you can talk to me, Florrie. And I wish you would."

Biting her lip, Florrie touched his arm. She talked to him all the time, loving their conversations, but she did always keep something back. Mostly because of how nervous she felt that this dream of hers would vanish and she would be back in the tenement she and Preston had been living in. She didn't want to have it snatched from her.

"You love me, don't you?"

He looked stunned at that.

"Of course I do! Why on earth would you say that?"

"Because I'm not of your social standing. I've got a lot of things that I still haven't dealt with. You must've been getting a lot of comments about marrying me, after all…"

"I have, and I don't care."

"But…"

Nolan shook his head.

"There are those who are shocked and confused why we got married, but if anyone has a problem with it and objects, they are out of my life. I'm not about to have anyone be disrespectful about my wedding and my wife." He touched her cheek, smiling fondly. "You're my main priority, Florrie. I love you, and I'm never going to change that. You don't have to worry about me in any capacity."

"But surely…" Florrie tried to insist. "Shutting people out of your social circle is detrimental to you? It's not a good idea to push them away if they're useful to your standing and your business."

"Not if it means making my wife miserable. If anyone disrespects you, they're not worth it." He shrugged. "I can manage. I can sort out the business in my own way, and things are going well. What I can't manage is not having you in my life. I want you there, and you need to be at my side. Nothing else matters."

Florrie felt her heart warm again. She had found it a little strange having someone declare their love for her so much, but she had gotten used to it. Now she enjoyed hearing Nolan speak about her in such a protective, loving tone.

It made her feel better, especially when she had a lower mood than usual. And with her sickness, that had been happening a lot lately.

"I think I should call for the doctor," Nolan said, pressing his fingers to her forehead. "Your cheek is cool, but your head is hot. And you look very pale."

"I was going to call in on him on my way to see Preston."

"You're not going anywhere, Florrie." His voice was firm, telling her he wouldn't take any sort of argument. "You're going to stay here and rest. I'll have the doctor come to us. He can look you over here."

Florrie wanted to argue, but she knew he wouldn't listen. She had to stay where she was and rest. Sighing, she nodded.

"All right. But will you stay with me?"

"If the doctor allows it. He might have to send me out of the room."

"I mean don't leave the house. I want you near."

Nolan smiled, and then he leaned over and kissed her.

"I'm not going anywhere, I promise." He stood up, squeezing her hand before letting go. "I'll get him now. Don't move from this bed, Florrie. You should try and get some sleep."

"I've been getting far too much of it lately."

He chuckled and headed towards the door.

"Make the most of it. You're likely not to have much soon."

He left, closing the door behind him, and Florrie was left wondering what he meant by that. Did he know something that she didn't?

Her hand went to her stomach again, pressing against it as it churned once more. She had thought about a reason for her not feeling well, but that was always in the back of her mind. She wanted to believe it was food poisoning first before considering the possibility that it might be something else. Something that only lasted a few months and resulted in a baby.

But she wasn't a doctor, and Florrie had never been pregnant. She didn't want to tell Nolan what she suspected and have him delighted, only to find out that wasn't the case. The doctor would need to be the one to tell him.

If she was pregnant, Florrie knew she would make sure that they didn't have the life she had growing up. They would be comfortable and happy for their whole lives. And that would make Florrie very happy, knowing she had done that for them.

Anything for her family.

CHAPTER 13

"I've been wondering where you went, Florence Walsh."

Florrie's heart sank when she heard a familiar voice. It had been one she hadn't heard in a long time; one she'd hoped would vanish and never come back again.

And of all the places to be, it had to be here?

Her heart pounding and feeling lightheaded, her chest tightening, Florrie looked up and saw Isadore Credge standing before her stall, giving her a smirk that looked triumphant and smug. Everyone around them carried on, not seeming to have noticed the moment and unaware of the atmosphere shifting.

Florrie hoped that someone would look over, to see how scared she was. She wanted to scream, but that stuck in her throat. And Credge was very good at bluffing; she had seen that from personal experience.

She needed to get out of there.

"Nothing to say?" Credge looked amused. "I was beginning to think you were going to give me some insolence as you've done before. You know how to talk back to me."

"What are you doing here?" Florrie squeaked and hated how weak she sounded.

"This is a charity event, isn't it? I'm just coming to contribute as one of their biggest benefactors."

Florrie thought she had misheard her. Her jaw dropped.

"You...you contribute to a charity to help struggling women in the city? And are they aware that you steal money from those trying to get out of poverty?"

Credge's eyes narrowed.

"I merely get what I'm owed, nothing more. And that's nothing to do with them."

"It's a bit of a contradiction in terms, isn't it?" Florrie shot back, now finding some of her courage. Her stomach felt like it was going to empty its contents, and she hoped she could aim it at Credge's nice dress. "You steal, and you know it. If you collected what you owed, then you would've left Preston and I alone."

"Your father didn't understand interest."

Florrie snorted.

"I understand interest, and that, at this point, you owe us. So how about you walk away and leave me alone before I let everyone know that you're more than willing to put struggling families into the workhouse because you care more about your personal wardrobe and bank account than you do about them."

Credge's cheeks flushed, and she looked Florrie up and down. Florrie wondered if she could tell that she was with child now. The confirmation from the doctor only the week before had made her feel like people could tell she was pregnant. She tried not to panic, hoping that Credge wouldn't somehow use that against her.

But that panic was making her courage build. She wasn't the little girl getting bullied by a woman anymore. She was grown, and she could go toe-to-toe with Credge now. She drew herself up to her full height.

"You're still young, Florence," Credge said. "You wouldn't understand."

"I understand that you should be sending my money back. At this point the lender is now the debtor." Florrie folded her arms. "You should've stopped years ago."

"I'm not giving you anything. You and your brother still owe me."

"Oh, we do? Would you like to say that a little louder and then everyone will know what you're really like."

Credge scoffed at that.

"You wouldn't dare humiliate yourself like that, would you? Everyone would know that you're in debt."

"As far as I'm concerned, I'm not. I'm just being harassed by a woman who has nothing better to do than to bully people."

"Is something wrong, Florrie?"

Florrie almost whimpered in relief when she heard Margaret's voice. Her mother-in-law approached and moved to stand at her side. She had been flitting around the various tables set out in the church hall, helping with the organising. Florrie wanted to hug her. Margaret looked from Florrie to Credge with a frown.

"You're looking rather distressed, dear."

"I'm just catching up with an old acquaintance," Credge said before Florrie could say anything. "I'm a friend of the family."

"Oh, really?"

From her expression, Margaret didn't believe that. She turned to Florrie, who decided to use this to her advantage.

"This is Isadore Credge. Father borrowed money from her, and she kept collecting, even after he died."

Credge's face went an even darker red. Margaret's eyebrows shot up.

"Oh, she did?"

"Despite the fact I'm sure we paid everything back; she's still demanding more from us. Even years later." Florrie fixed Credge with a pointed look. "She seems to think I'm stupid enough to think that this is a lifelong debt."

Credge looked as if she was going to have a fit. She spluttered. "That…what…what nonsense is this?"

"Florrie has made me aware of someone chasing her for money years after sorting out the debt, and how she and Preston were almost destitute because of that person's greed." Margaret's eyes narrowed at Credge. "So, it was you, was it? You're the one my daughter-in-law is trying to get away from?"

"Daughter-in-law?" Credge looked surprised. "You got married, Florence?"

"She did," Margaret spoke before Florrie could say anything. "And just because she's married into my family means you're not going to be taking any more money from her. In fact, I think this is about time we sorted out this 'debt' for good."

Credge's mouth opened and closed. It took her a moment to recover herself.

"But…the debt is still outstanding!" she protested. "I'm only getting back what I'm entitled to."

"I think there is something wrong with your records if you think that. How about we get my solicitor to contact you to sort this…debt out. I also have an accountant who works for my son's business. I will ask him to go through your records to make sure everything is up to date."

Credge looked incredulous. If she wasn't so flustered, Florrie would've burst out laughing at the sight.

"That's not necessary!" Credge cried. "I keep meticulous records, and I know what I'm owed."

"Then you won't have a problem with us confirming it, will you?" Margaret looked around the room. "Unless you want me to make a note in my speech later that it's nice we have a person collecting debts from the impoverished to keep her own pockets lined. I'm sure it won't go down well that you're here at a charity event for people who need financial and emotional support to live here in Manchester." Margaret tilted her head to one side as she regarded the other woman. "People are going to think you are looking for more potential…clients, so you can squeeze as much money out of them as possible."

Credge was bright red now, her eyes flaring in her outrage. Florrie had no idea how Margaret wasn't cowering before her; she felt like doing it.

"You wouldn't dare ruin a woman's business," Credge hissed. "I thought we were supposed to look out for each other."

"Not when you're bullying those who can't stand up to you." Margaret put a hand on Florrie's shoulder. "You're not going to do it to my daughter-in-law. And you can forget about coming after us for the money just because she's now married into a family with some wealth. You do that, and I'm sure you'll be the one owing us."

"Are you threatening me?"

"You came here to threaten Florrie, did you not? If you don't want me to threaten you in return, you shouldn't be doing it yourself."

Florrie was glad she had Margaret on her side; the woman was steely and formidable once she got going. Credge seemed to be realising that as well because she took a step back.

"I…I think I've come here under a misunderstanding," she mumbled.

"I wouldn't call it a misunderstanding." Margaret then called after her as Credge hurried towards the door. "My solicitor will be in contact with you to discuss our terms of agreement."

Florrie noticed people turning to stare at them and felt embarrassed. She ducked her head and turned away. Margaret squeezed her arm.

"I'm sorry about that, dear."

"I'm not ashamed of that. I just…"

"You didn't want anyone to know your business," Her mother-in-law finished for her. "We can keep it tactful, and if anyone asks you can be honest and say she's harassing you. From what you've told me about her; she likes to do it to those who can't afford a lawyer to tell her to back off."

Florrie had a feeling Credge had done it to more than just her. She had managed to get away from the woman for a couple of years and seeing her just now made her terrified it was going to happen again. This time, though, she had Margaret and Nolan. They were always going to look after her.

"Florrie!"

Turning, she saw her husband hurrying towards her. Florrie almost burst into tears at the sight of him. He wrapped her into his arms and hugged her tightly.

"I just saw someone leaving here muttering about a seamstress getting the better of her. I had a feeling she was talking about you." Nolan pulled back and searched her face with his eyes. "Was that her? The woman you told me about?"

Florrie couldn't answer. She just nodded. Nolan groaned and hugged her again, kissing her head.

"I'm sorry I wasn't here for you. I should've put her in her place."

"I had your mother here as well." Florrie pulled back and managed a smile. "She put Credge's nose out of joint, and it was a joy to witness."

She had been a little put out in the beginning, when Nolan had told his mother about the situation without letting Florrie know that he was doing it. She had been annoyed that he would do that without thinking, but Margaret had been very understanding. Apparently, it wasn't the first time she had heard of this happening. Florrie was shocked that someone could continue as they did and not care about who they were hurting.

"Why don't you take Florrie home, Nolan?" Margaret suggested. "She's had a shock, and I think she needs the rest."

"Yes, Mother."

"Make sure she puts her feet up and has a strong cup of tea."

Margaret gave Florrie a knowing look. "And some sugar, but not too much."

"I'll sort that out," Nolan called over his shoulder as he led Florrie towards the door.

She was still confused as to what the older woman meant by that. Something in her tone suggested that she knew something. She frowned at Nolan as they stepped outside into the crisp afternoon air.

"What was going on there?"

"Hmm?"

"She was talking as if she knew something." Florrie put a hand on her still-flat stomach. "Do you think she knows?"

Nolan smiled and shook his head.

"I shouldn't think so. We were going to wait a few more weeks before we said anything, weren't we?"

"But she's a shrewd woman. She likely figured something out." Florrie peered at her husband. "Unless you said something? I know how excited you were when I told you the doctor confirmed it."

He held up his hands.

"I never said a word! I'm not about to ruin the moment. But she might've heard how excited I was. If you recall, she came into the room not long after you told me."

Florrie suspected that could be it. She couldn't see Margaret listening at keyholes, but it wouldn't surprise her if this was what happened. She didn't mind Margaret knowing - she was fond of the woman - but she wanted to keep the secret to herself a little longer.

"I hope that's the case, and she's not going to start taking over." She leaned into him. "I know she's not like that, but there's still that worry."

"You don't need to worry about anything when it comes to my mother," Nolan said with a smile, putting his arm around her and kissing her head. "She's a solid, reliable woman. I know you see that."

"You understand my trust…"

"I do, and you don't need to remind me. But you know that Mother will do anything to protect you. I think she loves you more than she does me. Don't be surprised if she treats you more like her child than me."

Florrie thought about what happened with Credge, and the interaction between the two women. Margaret had defended her, and she was more than prepared to fight her corner. She had no doubt about how protective her mother-in-law was. And for someone who was not on the same level as her son in the beginning.

When she showed how much she cared, it really came through. She had been incredibly lucky with it.

CHAPTER 14

"You're pregnant?" Preston stared at her with wide eyes. "You're serious?"

Biting her lip, Florrie nodded.

"Nolan and I have told Margaret, and we wanted to tell you before we let anyone else aware of it."

"You...you're..." Preston looked stunned, swaying on his feet. "I can't believe you're telling me you're going to become a mother."

"Neither am I." Florrie rested a hand on her belly, nervous about his response. She had hoped her brother would be happy about it, but he seemed to be in shock. "You're not upset, are you?"

"No, of course not!" He shook himself before smiling and hugging her. "Sorry, I was just stunned. When you asked me over, I never thought you'd say you were going to have a baby. I thought it was something else."

She laughed.

"Like what?"

"I don't know, but certainly not that." Preston eased back, his smile fading a little. "I mean, Nolan did make me aware that

Credge had come to you a few days ago, and you were rather shaken. There was a chance it was about that."

Florrie had been trying to get that interaction out of her head. She certainly didn't like reliving it, especially when she remembered the way Credge looked at her with a sneer. She had been intending to humiliate Florrie somehow, and she knew making a fuss would draw attention. But she hadn't planned for it to be turned on her. Margaret had done that beautifully.

Who would've thought that Credge wasn't happy about being called out for her bullying ways? If she was taking money from people, she must've been called several unflattering names. It had to come with the job, although Credge treated it like a pastime, as far as Florrie could tell. It must be how she had very nice clothes.

"What are we going to do about that?" Preston asked, watching her with a frown. "Are we going to have to deal with her again? I'm not running, not after everything we've done."

"I'm not running, either," Florrie said firmly. "Nolan and Margaret said they would be dealing with it. I'm not going to argue with them about it. It's something to leave alone."

"Even though I can tell you're itching to sort it out yourself?"

"It is our problem, after all. It's something we should look after, but..." She shrugged. "Nolan and Margaret were adamant about leaving it to them. And they're our family now, so we should trust them with it."

Preston's expression said otherwise. He wasn't entirely sure. Florrie could see his side; they were handing over the dealings they had been handling for years to someone else. Even though he liked Nolan and Margaret, and they treated him like they'd known him for years, he still had problems trusting.

She was in the same boat. She was getting better at trusting, but with someone like Credge...

A door somewhere in the house opened and closed a little too quickly, the noise making both jump. Florrie hurried to the window and looked out, wondering if someone had left the house in a hurry. Nolan's carriage was outside, pulling away slowly. He must've come back from wherever he went.

A moment later, Nolan and Margaret entered the morning room, both looking triumphant. Florrie could feel the mood lifting as they came in. Margaret beamed when she saw Preston.

"Preston, dear! How are you?" She clasped Preston's hands. "You're looking well, although you look as if you need more sleep."

Preston chuckled.

"Much as I'd like to sleep for a week, I can't really afford it."

"Well, why don't you and I go and see if we can get a tray of tea and cake for us? We can leave Nolan and Florrie alone." Margaret winked at Florrie. "I think husband and wife have a lot to talk about."

Florrie was confused. What was going on? She barely got a chance to say anything in response before her mother-in-law was leaving, practically tugging Preston behind her. She turned to Nolan, who just watched her with a smile.

"What's going on? I'm getting concerned now."

"You don't need to be concerned about anything." Nolan approached her, pulling her into his arms and kissing her. "Everything's been sorted. You don't have to worry about Credge anymore."

That got her attention, but before Florrie could speak, he led her over to the settee and sat her down, settling beside her and taking her hand.

"We took our accountant and solicitor over to Credge's residence. Her husband let us in, very confused as to what we were up to."

"What? She's married?"

"You didn't know?"

Florrie frowned.

"I suppose I must've heard it some years ago, but I've always known her as Credge. I can't see her having a husband, not with that personality."

Nolan grunted.

"We were surprised that he was around as well, but it made getting to look at Credge's accounts a lot easier. Apparently, her husband had no idea that she was even doing this."

"What? Really?"

"No idea at all. He had been told that Credge was tapping into a trust fund a distant relative had left her, so that was the reason for all the nice clothes and going out all the time. To hear it was to collect money for supposed debts after she leant it out was a shock. Especially when it was his money she was using for that."

Florrie's head was spinning. She had known that the woman would need access to money in the first place to lend, but to do it with her husband's money and he didn't know about it was startling. How had he not noticed?

"And so, when the debtor paid off the debt, that went back to the husband's account?"

"Yes, but she always put on hefty interest so she could get something for herself. And if she saw the person in question as a soft touch and easy to manipulate, she kept doing it."

"Which is what she was doing to me and Preston," Florrie said bitterly. "We were children, and she was exploiting us."

"Pretty much." Nolan scowled, his fingers tightening around hers. "I can't believe that happened to you. It's so shocking that she would do that to children, especially when you needed every penny you could."

Florrie had suspected it for years, but hearing this confirmed it all. Isadore Credge was ice-cold, and she didn't care who she hurt in the process. She wished that she could go to the woman and slap her smug face, but that would only be momentary satisfaction. She wasn't about to bother with that.

"What happened when you looked at her books?" she asked. "Did you find anything?"

"Plenty. And we found your name in the books. Your debt is about ten times bigger than it was when your father took out the money. He would've paid it all back by the time he died with just one payment left, but Credge didn't write it off. She just kept going."

Florrie felt lightheaded. They had been paying off a non-existent debt? How did Credge justify that? That was far more than just paying interest.

"I...what...I don't know what's going on anymore."

"It's not just you that she's done that to." Nolan's tone was grim. "She's been doing this for fifteen years, since before she married her husband."

"Where was she getting the money before?"

"From her father. He didn't seem to know, either. Credge was very good at making herself look sweet and innocent around those she needed the money from. She had a double life going on, and it worked for her for years."

"Oh, my," Florrie murmured. "All she cared about was the money."

"She thought it was a good way to get money of her own, not caring that she was stealing from others and making them struggle. I shudder to think how many people have ended up destitute because of her."

"What did her husband say about it?"

Nolan gave her a wry smile. He looked exhausted, but the delight in his eyes still danced through.

"He was shocked, to say the least. He couldn't believe that he had been married to someone who would steal. He's a big philanthropist, so to see the proof that his wife was taking from those he often tried to help had to be a big blow to him. He looked ready to explode as we left."

Florrie felt a stab of sympathy for Credge's husband. She was sure he had no idea about it, and it would be a shock to anyone if they had someone they loved betray them. She hoped that he would do something about it. Credge deserved to have the money cut off from her.

She sighed, twisting her fingers in Nolan's hand as she absently pressed a hand to her stomach.

"I suppose it's too much to ask if she's going to end up in prison or something. She's part of the upper class, isn't she?"

"I think that will be decided, but if she doesn't, she'll be incredibly lucky." Nolan leaned in and rested his forehead against hers. "You don't need to worry about any of that now, though. She's out of our lives, and she's never going to bother you again."

"I hope so."

"I know so. I made a point of telling her never to darken our family again, otherwise I'll be bringing legal action against her. My solicitor made sure to give her and Mr Credge a document reiterating it all."

Florrie felt something she hadn't experienced in a long time. A weight lifting off her shoulders. It felt good, and she swayed where she sat. Nolan put an arm around her.

"Are you all right, Florrie?"

"I can't believe this is happening. That I'm going to finally be rid of her." Florrie swallowed. "I was so worried she would be bothering me until my dying days."

"Not while I'm around. I'm not letting her anywhere near you." Nolan pressed his hand over hers on her stomach. "I love you, Florrie. I will protect you for as long as I live. Especially against disgusting creatures like Isadore Credge."

Florrie knew that. She believed that she was safe now. Nolan had promised that on their wedding day, and he had never failed her. She kissed him, pulling back with a smile.

"I love you, too. And I'm so glad you came into my life."

Nolan grinned, kissing her forehead.

"I'm more than glad I was the one who went to get Uncle's trousers that day. It's the best decision I ever made."

EPILOGUE

*S*ix *Months Later*

"Careful, Florrie!" Margaret hurried over to her, looking horrified. "You shouldn't be doing that in your condition!"

Florrie laughed, putting the pile of clothes onto the table between them.

"I'm pregnant, Margaret. I'm not ill or disabled. I'm perfectly fine."

"Even so..."

"Weren't you telling me about how much you did when you were pregnant, and it didn't do you any harm?"

Margaret sighed.

"I did that until the final month of pregnancy. I didn't want to move around too much or be away from home when I went into labour. Up until then, I was active, but not at the point you are. And you're due to give birth in a week."

"You don't need to worry about me. This little one is quite content." Florrie pressed a hand to her swollen belly. "It feels solid, and I can feel them settling on the bottom of my stomach, but it's nothing I can't manage."

Margaret gave Nolan a pleading look, her son sat on the settee by the window with the newspaper. He laughed.

"Don't look at me, Mother. She wants to be the one who moves around when she should be resting."

"But even so…"

"Maybe it might make labour easier on her?" Nolan suggested. "The doctor did say the more active a pregnant woman is, the easier the pregnancy. Might as well find out."

Margaret pursed her lips.

"As long as she doesn't take a step sideways and give birth right then."

"That's not going to happen!"

"Knowing you two, I wouldn't be surprised."

Florrie laughed, setting about folding the clothes in front of her. She was getting them ready for the next charity event, sorting them out for those who were in more need than her. So many people were happy to donate, and she was grateful for that. It was a relief that they had so many generous neighbours and those willing to help, even in the smallest of ways. She could already see those who needed it lighting up in delight at the spoils before them.

Having been there herself, she knew how much that would mean to them. Florrie wished she'd had people like her neighbours. She had Mr and Mrs Irons, a few old neighbours, but there was only so much they could do. None of them have a woman like Credge chasing them for money she didn't deserve.

She did sometimes think about what was going on with that woman. Was she in prison? Or had she left London in disgrace? It would be a relief not to bump into her or be looking over her shoulder.

"Is Preston coming over later?" Margaret asked as she began to fold clothes alongside Florrie. "He mentioned something last time, but I can't remember it entirely."

"He was coming to dinner tonight." Florrie smiled. "I think he wants to introduce his new lady friend."

"Oh?"

"He's been mentioning a girl who works in the house as a kitchen maid. They end up talking a lot when she's in the garden picking vegetables, and I know they've gone out together on their afternoons off."

Florrie had found it sweet when Preston confessed to her what was going on in his private life. His face had been bright red, embarrassed to admit it, but Florrie knew he was pleased. He had found someone who liked him, even after telling her about what he did as a child. She wasn't judgemental at all.

It was adorable, and she was glad he was finding happiness himself.

"I'm interested to see who has caught his eye," Margaret said with a sly smile. "It's not often I see him going shy over someone."

"Same here." Florrie jumped when Nolan barked out a laugh, almost one of triumph. "Nolan, please! Don't scare me like that!"

"Sorry, love. But I just read this, and I couldn't help myself." Nolan looked up from the paper as he sat up, his eyes wide. "Isadore Credge has been convicted. It's been announced today."

Margaret heaved a sigh of relief.

"Thank God for that! I thought they were taking forever to come to a decision. We were in court weeks ago."

"Only two weeks ago, Margaret," Florrie pointed out.

"It shouldn't take that long to come to a decision."

"I suppose someone was ill, and they had to wait for them to recover. That normally happens." Nolan stood and brought the newspaper over, laying it on the table. "She's been convicted of theft, among other things. She's going to prison."

Florrie leaned over his arm and read the article herself.

"There's a comment from her husband. Are they still married?"

"I believe it's in the works to divorce her. And you know how hard it is to get a divorce nowadays."

"He's got reason for it this time, though."

Nolan nodded.

"Then he should be a free man soon. He's going to be finally rid of her." He put his arm around Florrie. "At least that woman will never darken our doorstep again. She's going to be away for a few years, and I doubt she'll want to come back and get humiliated when everyone knows what she's done. She's a proud woman, so that would be out of the question."

"So that means I'm free," Florrie murmured.

"You are." Her husband kissed her head. "You're free, Florrie. For good."

She slumped against him, hugging him tightly. Margaret grinned.

"Which means nothing holding you back anymore, Florence. You can do whatever you want."

"I can." Florrie winked at her. "And I think I'm going to take your advice and sit down. I'm about to give birth, after all. I shouldn't be overdoing it."

Margaret groaned, but soon all three of them were laughing. And it felt like the best sound Florrie had ever heard.

The End

IF YOU ENJOYED THIS STORY, could I please ask you to leave a review on Amazon?

Thank you so much.

Printed in Dunstable, United Kingdom